Chindi

CHINDI

Copyright © 2021 by Timothy Bryan

First published in the United States 2021

Printed in the United States of America

Chindi

By
Timothy Bryan

*How we shall laugh at the
trouble of parting when we
meet again!*

-Henry Scott Holland,
Death is Nothing at all

Table of Contents

Chapter 1

Northeastern California, Fall 1862

A gentle river cut through an open meadow in a remote valley of far-northeastern California. Clumps of rough grass and scattered trees swayed near the waterway's edge, gently moving with a low-howling wind.

The horizon was dominated by snow-tipped mountain peaks, and dark clouds spilled over their snowy crests in a roiling wave, making the incoming weather system appear hostile to the lonely fields surrounding the river.

In the rippling water stood a weathered man, one whose stooped bearing and leathery skin made him oddly appropriate to the scene. With frayed suspenders and an untucked shirt, Abraham looked the part of a worn prospector toiling at the edge of the known world.

Jerking upright, Abraham sloshed toward the muddy riverbank, struggling with an arthritic gait through the frigid stream. With a determined grimace, he grunted at the effort of carrying a dirt-filled bucket, and his cracked lips, barely visible under his ratty beard, pursed in a concentrated scowl.

Abraham approached a rocker box on the shore, lifting his bucket to dump soil into the wooden apparatus. Designed to allow dirt to be sifted in an efficient manner, Abraham began his gold-hunting task, methodically sluicing through sand and gravel in the weathered box.

Though aged, Abraham's eyes were also eager—youthful even. His face was that of an expectant gambler, always betting on the long shot, despite his body having to pay the price for the failed betting endeavor.

"Billy, what's the chances we got a good location fer the gold?" Abraham asked.

A short distance away stood his brother Billy. Billy was a few years younger than his upper-fifties brother, but his appearance matched that of his sibling, both from genetics and occupation.

Billy straightened himself from a hole he had been digging and mopped his brow with a tattered rag taken from a patched pocket. In his other hand, he balanced a crude pick against the rocky ground.

"It's a good location for us, and it don't look like nobody's been here before," said Billy, and his more restrained expression also showed excitement. Gold fever affected everyone, and the only difference among brothers was a matter of degree.

Abraham nodded in agreement, and his bobbing head resumed its stare at the soil below. His face glowed with energy, and with each word his enthusiasm grew. "I never thought we'd get this all to ourselves."

It became quiet for a moment, and each man fell into his own thoughts. Billy began breaking up the dirt with his pick, scowling down with each grunting swing, while Abraham's eyes scoured the wet soil for evidence of gold in the middle of his muddied wooden tray.

Glancing conspiratorially toward the distant Sierra Nevada Mountains, Abraham's self-motivation subsided, and he lowered his voice as he pondered the uninhabited area around them. "Yeah, we lucky fer sure, but we just gotta to watch out for dem savages. They'd just as soon gut ya as look at ya."

Tilting his head doubtfully, Billy shook his head in response. His face was marred by gaps in his rotten teeth, but the effect was offset by his friendly features and happy-to-please smile.

"Nah. I was at the fort a week ago, and they wasn't worryin' about the Injuns. Said they been less mean lately. Said they came to an understandin' with the army."

Stopping, Billy thought for a moment, then reconsidered the prospect of danger. Patting a large revolver stuffed into his filthy clothing, his eyes grew more serious. "But ye can't be too careful. No such thing as being too careful."

Nodding intently, Abraham returned to his dirt box. Forgetting his brief concern for safety, he focused instead on the business of getting rich as he shook the soil around inside the contraption.

Billy went back to enlarging the ditch near the riverbank, and the wet soil crumbled with each whack of his tool. Filling up several more buckets, he ferried more sludge to Abraham's box.

The brothers made quite a team, and in no time, Billy's hole grew to a deepening trench. Loose dirt and sand collected around the duo as they sorted attentively for traces of the precious metal.

Billy continued chipping away at the soil, until a *thunk* announced something new in the ground. With confused eyes, Billy stared into the muddy mess and called out to his brother.

"Abraham, I got somethin' here."

Several more strikes with the pick brought the same sound. Peering down expectantly, Billy motioned again to his brother. "Yeah, somethin' here—for sure."

Intrigued, Abraham wandered over to the trench to look. Staring down, he was skeptical, and he arched an eyebrow when Billy motioned for him to check it out.

After considering a moment, Abraham jumped down. Reaching deep into the squishy earth, the sludgy soil went halfway up his exposed arms. He grimaced as he searched through the muck, grasping for the source of the strange sound.

With a triumphant grunt, Abraham yanked free a satchel of some kind. Covered in a mire of brown earth, he grasped the outside, trying to scrub it clean. Giving up, he gestured to the water in the river's shallows, indicating he would wash off the excess crud.

"Looks like some sorta saddlebag. I can't rightly tell. It's got somethin' inside, too," said Abraham.

Trudging into the river, Abraham scraped away grime from the bag with his trembling fingers. It was some kind of Indian satchel with strips of sinewy leather hanging from it. As he cleaned away the crusted outside, artwork became visible, and Abraham smiled as he scoured away the rest of the mud.

Images of men with spears and buffalo were burned into the bag, and a bizarre whitish-painted figure stood in the middle of the ancient artistry. The figure looked human, like the rest of the stenciled Native Americans represented there, but its color and proportion were different.

"Maybe we found some kinda treasure someone buried. Can you imagine how rich we gonna get?" Abraham asked, wrestling with the bag in the cold water.

Confused, Billy gazed at his brother's back, appearing less enthusiastic as Abraham stopped talking. In fact, Abraham stopped moving entirely as he continued staring down at the wet bag in his hands.

Billy couldn't see what Abraham saw, and he moved to the side to get a better view. "Well, what the hell is it?"

With no response forthcoming, Billy shrugged and moved back to his trench. Abraham was still quiet as Billy resumed digging.

After several more strikes, another odd sound came from the ditch, and this time it was solid—maybe metallic.

Ignoring his still-idle brother, Billy hopped into the ditch. Reaching down, he slid his fingers under the wet dirt, grasping something hard and cold with both hands. He became confused as he felt around in the mud, trying to figure out what the new object could be. Pulling hard, Billy grunted from the effort, but it was thoroughly stuck in the clodded earth, as if it was fused into the deep soil.

As Billy continued tugging, Abraham's shadow moved next to Billy on the trench floor.

With a final yank, Billy pulled out a horrific human skull from the mucky ground. Several vertebrae were still attached to the fetid head, and gray flesh clung in strips to its bony exterior.

Landing on his ass, Billy's shocked face was matched by his shrill voice. He threw the skull far way, half expecting it to bite him. "What the hell is this? Abraham, why are ye just standing there? Help me outta here."

Struggling to turn around, Billy worked his way to his knees in the sludge. Glaring up at his unseen brother, his expression changed to one of sheer terror. Quivering in shock, he struggled to understand what he was looking at, and he stuttered out a series of nonsensical words.

"Ahhhhh...no...no, what is...you...?"

Billy screamed. His tortured and hysterical wails went on and on, like a man whose mind was being eaten from within.

From high above, the meandering river crossed the beautiful meadow, snaking its way toward the distant and striking mountain range. Billy's terrified shrieks carried across that remote landscape, until they turned to incoherent babbling—and then to no sound at all.

#

A pleasant meadow lay recessed and surrounded by forest on all sides. A narrow trail led downhill toward the wide grasslands, and farther across the open field were a series of huts making up a small village. Above, cloudy skies cast shaded light over the gloomy landscape.

Chief Hakan leaned against a tree near the trail, staring out over the open space below. Looking worried and disturbed, he was a formidable man, well-built and used to the rigors of living in the harsh elements. Streaks of gray ran through his hair, and coupled with his deep worry lines, showed a man accustomed to stoicism and loss.

"Where are the braves? And the women and children?" Hakan asked, frustrated, as his eyes darted about.

On the field, there was no evidence of life. No sounds or movement emerged from the small village—it was completely quiet.

It was an unnatural silence, one that didn't fit the backdrop of what should have been a lively camp. Fire pits spaced between the huts showed no smoke. Children didn't play among their homes, and women didn't tend to bowls of porridge or other duties that encompassed the daily lives of his people.

Silah met Hakan's gaze. Equally troubled, the young Indian shook his head. Moving his tomahawk in proficient loops at his side, he motioned to a group of braves behind him. The young warriors crept down the trail, advancing toward the field and small village.

As they moved across the open meadow, the eyes of each man scanned warily. No movement caught their attention, and no friend emerged to greet them. It was as if nobody had ever lived in the familiar surroundings, and each warrior's mood darkened.

As the long grass parted ahead of them, Silah raised his weapon. Other braves did the same, and every step forward brought the chance of conflict from some as-yet-unknown foe.

Yet no enemy awaited them. They stepped carefully to the outskirts of the settlement, and everything was still and silent. Standing with a confused gaze, Silah motioned back to Hakan that the way was clear.

Hakan paced toward the warriors, stopping to look at tracks on the ground as his men entered the huts. Placing his fingers on indentations in the dirt, he examined their size and depth. The ground showed tracks and prints, indicating a wide variety of feet had walked in the upturned earth.

Perplexed, Hakan rose and glanced up to the overcast sky. Licking his lips, his watery eyes scanned the surrounding foliage; he was looking for something, hoping for another clue for what had transpired here.

Silah emerged from one of the huts. Looking even more concerned than before, the young warrior also surveyed the surrounding area carefully. He hurried to Hakan and gestured to their surroundings.

"Nobody is here. There is blood everywhere. Where could they have gone? Maybe it was a raid?"

Sighing, Hakan motioned to the tracks. His voice lowered, and it was full of dread and worry. "These were not made by the moccasins of our people. They were made by the stiff shoes of the white man. At least, a few of them."

From the distance, a whistle came from one of his men. Chatan, another young warrior, ran from one of the huts, his eyes betraying panic. The young brave motioned to Hakan and pointed to the entrance.

Striding up to the hut, Hakan cast the curtain aside.

Inside were the corpses of a family. A brave lay sprawled there, draped across the bodies of his wife and child. There were multiple bullet holes in his back, as if he died trying to shield his family.

The dead man still clutched a knife, defiant to the end. Around the bodies were clothing and personal items, including a crude doll and beaded jewelry. Staples of food were stacked to the back of the hut, piled high for storage to endure the long winter.

"If it was a raid, why are the food supplies untouched?" asked Hakan, "The Paiute do not leave food to rot, and they are no friends of the white man."

Hakan faced away from the tragic scene. His angry features grew more intense with each passing moment, and as he paced away from the murdered family, his gaze jumped to each of his concerned warriors.

Hakan looked deeply into each man's eyes and offered a consoling nod of shared grief. The returned gazes from his men were filled with outrage and a desire for vengeance as their anxious eyes sought the cause of the massacre.

With the collection of fighting men processing their sorrow, a pained silence filled the air of the now-empty village.

Considering the horrid events that surrounded them, Hakan stewed in raw emotions as he came to grips with the needless slaughter of his tribe. Raising his voice and trying to control the rage in his trembling jaw, he was just able to croak his words out.

"They are attacking us again. But why?"

Chapter 2

Dust blew down the trail in a great gout, making it difficult to see. Surrounding the high-mountain path were fields of dirty grass, with scraggly trees spaced throughout the isolated terrain.

In the sky, fading light cast elongated shadows across distant barren hills. The day was waning, and the dust storm limited visibility even further.

It was not a welcoming environment.

Lieutenant George Crook crouched in the wind, holding his hat in place. As the minor gale died down, he stood, looking confused at tracks on the ground. His earnest face was framed by an exquisite beard, one that needed great care to cultivate and maintain. Of medium build, he was a man that exuded confidence, despite his average frame. Studying the surrounding environment, his proper bearing was officious and rigid.

"Mr. Pugh, what do you make of the tracks? It would appear they are truly of the Hewisidawi?" Crook asked, using the local term for the nearby Indian tribe.

Standing farther down the trail, scout William Pugh considered the question. Dressed in simple trail clothing, he looked at place in the remote surroundings, and a plug of tobacco leaked dark juice into his tangled whiskers, completing his gruff appearance.

Pugh raised his voice to be heard over the distant wail of wind. "Can't say that I understand why they're moving about, Lieutenant. They were in a hurry; that much is certain."

"They are not seeking to hide their intrusion, which is a great concern," replied Crook. "I had hoped this sort of behavior to be something of the past."

Pugh merely nodded, spitting absently to the side. He moved his gaze across the shrubbery and brush, looking for further signs of movement.

Behind Pugh, three more soldiers sat perched on horses. Their uniforms were grimy, and their faces were fatigued in the failing light. Scanning the area with disinterested frowns, their lack of enthusiasm was palpable, and they took turns avoiding Crook's stern and demanding glare.

At the back of the column sat Sergeant Lorenzo Loraine, who shifted uncomfortably in his saddle. The noncommissioned officer was middle-aged but strapping. A bull of a man, his skeptical features lent intelligence to his otherwise intimidating posture. In his cheek, he turned over his own chaw of tobacco, slurping on the leafy mix.

"Lieutenant, I don't like the look of this. They've been keeping to themselves for a year. Now they up and start trouble around the ranches?"

Crook spent some time considering Loraine's words. Visibly perplexed, he transferred his gaze down the trail. "I also am of the belief that this is not a fortuitous sign, Sergeant Loraine. When one breaks his promises, it usually bodes ill for future relations, especially in a time when we are seeking to build trust."

Sighing, Crook mounted his horse and surveyed their surroundings. He focused down the trail, paying particular attention to the hills that stood aside their path. Their way ahead was precarious, as it skirted below multiple defensive outcroppings.

"Mr. Pugh, please proceed cautiously as we continue our pursuit of the Indians," Crook said. "There exists an opportunity for ambush due to those elevated ridges. We may have to pull back if engaged from such a commanding position."

Pugh nodded and followed Crook's gaze, squinting into the late afternoon light. Mounting his horse in a skilled manner, he kicked it into a slow trot to lead the group.

As Pugh steered his horse down the darkening path, he called back over his shoulder. "Will do, Lieutenant. Something's got them stirred up, and they're unpredictable when that happens."

Pugh led the column of soldiers forward, focusing on hills to either side of the trail as he gingerly picked his way ahead. His cautious bearing was infectious, and the others trailed carefully behind him.

#

Pugh took a deep and sad breath, raising his face to the darkening sky. The clouds above churned and roiled, much like his own distraught internal considerations. Heartbroken, his teary eyes darted about, and he didn't know what to do or say. Turning to the rest of the party, he exhaled slowly to settle his nerves.

Below him, Private Selby lay dead on the trail. On his back, the soldier had his arms outstretched, as if begging when death came for him.

Selby's pupils were cloudy white, and a layer of dust coated his face, making his death-pose complexion oddly dark. A handful of arrows protruded from his chest, announcing the source of his violent demise.

The area surrounding the group was full of thorns and bright shrubbery. The path moving ahead proceeded through pine trees and manzanita bushes, which were barely visible in the failing light. The dense foliage was shadowed and impenetrable to the naked eye, offering ample opportunities for ambush or discrete observation by any potential enemy.

Overcoming his grief, Pugh leveled his eyes at Crook. "Well, this seals it. Selby left for Fort Bidwell three days ago, and his body appears dead exactly that long. They left him to rot."

Around the scene, the other mounted soldiers faced outward, ready for any further attack. Each of the distressed troopers had his musket raised and eyes alert, prepared for the worst.

Moving forward, Crook bent over the corpse, studying it intently. Looking at the ground next to the body, he examined nearby tracks in the upturned earth. He appeared noncommittal, almost clinical, as he took in the tragic scene and silently counted the tracks of the attackers.

"Yes, that would appear to be the case. However, the other tracks we are following are not so old," said Crook.

Crook walked farther down the trail, scanning the ground in intervals and making mental calculations concerning the events that surrounded Selby's death.

"That would indicate a separate party is involved," Crook said. "Meaning at least two bands are about making mischief. Two potential sources of conflict—and two causes for concern."

Pugh shook his head, appearing stumped. "But that makes no sense, Lieutenant. They've been peaceful lately, even accommodating. Why risk the punishment they'll surely get from this?"

Abruptly, Loraine dismounted. Walking to the dead man, he crossed himself and bowed his head in prayer. With sad eyes and a somber voice, he motioned to the corpse. "Selby was a good man, Lieutenant. I should cover him...to take him back to the fort."

Nodding, Crook gestured to one of the horses. "Yes, please do so, Sergeant. Pack his body on the spare horse. We can offer him a proper burial there."

The party went quiet as Loraine covered the body. It took a while for him to tie it up for transport, and when Loraine slung him over the horse, the bloated corpse squished as he cinched it down. Even with his iron jaw, Loraine struggled against the odor from the deceased man.

More silence came from each of the companions as they locked eyes. Sadness and despair radiated from the group as they contemplated who could be next to have their earthly remains prepared for transport over a horse.

Serving in the army on the frontier meant such an end was always a possibility, but the sudden occurrence of a violent end to someone they had known personally brought the reality too close for personal comfort.

Stepping close to Pugh, Crook lowered his voice and gestured vaguely into the night. "We shall have to check on the Scott family at their ranch while in this area."

Looking doubtful, Pugh peered into the encroaching darkness. He matched Crook's low tone and pointed to the north.

"Lieutenant Crook, it'll be dark soon. Be dangerous to travel at night, especially now."

"Indeed it will, Mr. Pugh, but the civilians we are charged to protect will not have the luxury of waiting for us in the morning. Our charter to ensure the safety of the local settlers is more important than ever in such a precarious time."

Pugh nodded at the gentle reminder of their duties, but he didn't hide his doubts. Being a treasured civilian scout attached to the regular army allowed him leeway in dealing with the government's rigid command structure, and he always felt it his duty to be forthright, especially with an officer like Crook—one who appreciated honesty.

Turning to peer up at the rest of the group, Crook gathered himself, glancing at each of his anxious men in turn. He raised his voice, trying to keep his tone determined and fearless.

"Men, please ready yourselves for conflict. I fear it will be waiting for us in the near future, and we must be prepared for it."

#

Moonlight made visibility tolerable, highlighting a lonely ranch house. No light escaped from the simple building, and its windows were dark outlines against its log exterior. A covered front porch ran the length of the front of the home.

On the porch lay an unmoving body, but it was too dark to determine the corpse's identity. Lying on its face, the sprawled dark shape gave the impression of trying to look through the porch's floorboards.

A corral with cows was penned to the side of structure, and a large barn stood behind the cattle. The animals were quiet as they stood in the enclosed space, while an unseen horse neighed from somewhere deep inside the barn.

Lt. Crook crouched behind a pasture gate, trying to keep his silhouette hidden from detection. Staring at the building and clutching his revolver, he waited for someone to show themselves.

Watching for some time, Crook glanced between the building and the barn. Nobody emerged, and he frowned while he considered the situation.

Behind him, Loraine and another soldier also crouched low, holding their muskets down to avoid marking their position. Breathing as quietly as possible, they gazed expectantly at Crook.

"You enter the front of the house, while I will come from the back," whispered Crook. "Wait until my signal before making entry."

"Are you sure that's wise?" replied Loraine in an equally low tone. "The Scotts have a young daughter."

Crook shot Loraine an impatient gaze, one that was only partially obscured by the darkness. He waved his revolver in the general direction of the dark house.

"Yes, Sergeant, I'm painfully aware of that fact. But if we chatter here instead of going to her rescue, we might well be unhappy with the result."

Thinking it over, Loraine nodded and motioned to the soldier behind him. Together they sneaked through the hazy night toward the building, pausing at times to ensure their silence as they advanced toward the porch.

Gathering his courage, Crook detached from the fence and made his own way around the building. Stepping carefully, he avoided disturbing the cows as he slipped through another fence and skirted the side of the house.

Each step was careful and controlled, and Crook's intense eyes scoured each corner and nook of the structures. Moving cautiously, he proceeded with precision to a good vantage point at the back of the house.

The view of the back door was excellent. Crook waited, breathing in gasps as he scanned the surrounding property.

Crook's gaze returned on the rear of the structure, and he focused intently on the shadowed back door of the ranch home, even while he struggled to control his anxiety at what was coming next.

Some time passed.

With some skill, Crook made an owl-whistle, which was soon followed by his men kicking in the front door. As they banged around the front of the building, a man appeared at the back door, carrying a torch and preparing to exit.

The man was a Native, and the bare-chested Indian paused at the rear window, considering his options. He soon barged out the back door and rushed for the safety of the woods beyond.

"Halt," commanded Crook, and he scrambled to stop the man from escaping.

Pointing his revolver at the Native's chest, Crook saw a formidable adversary. The man was covered in blood, and his side pouch only partially hid the remnants of a dangling scalp. The Indian held out the torch, and his hateful glare focused entirely on Crook.

"Stop, or I will shoot you where you stand," shouted Crook.

Crook's opponent paused, unsure of what to do next. Moments passed.

With a flick of his wrist, the Native cast the torch at Crook. Crook fired high while ducking the fire, whereas the Native charged low, avoiding the shot.

They embraced in a stand-up struggle, with the Indian grabbing Crook's wrist, while Crook grasped his enemy's other knife-wielding hand.

The combatants stared at each other in a test of strength. The Native growled, his vengeful glare focused and bitter. Crook tried to grab the man's hair, but the warrior stopped him with his powerful grasp, forcing Crook to drop the revolver as he twisted his arm backward.

Crook was being overpowered, and he stumbled back before his stronger opponent. The Native inverted his knife and pressed it toward Crook's front leg. The tip of the knife pressed forward, piercing the thick woolen material of his pants.

The knife's point slowly stabbed into Crook's thigh, and his pants turned red with his soaking blood. Grunting, Crook fell to his knees, then his back.

The Indian climbed on top of Crook as he fell backward, punctuating his impending victory with a spiteful grin. The look of ravenous anticipation at slaying his hated opponent filled the warrior's expression with glowing assertiveness and exhilaration.

As his death seemed imminent, Crook used his last strength to push up the Native, creating some space between them.

The sound of a musket shot matched exactly with the Native's jaw being blown from his face, and the man tumbled over. Gore splattered across Crook's eyes as the Native crumpled to the side.

Crook blinked under the deluge of blood covering his face. Rising to sit, he saw that death was no longer imminent, but he didn't register why.

Running at Crook, holding his rifled musket in one hand and reaching out with the other, Loraine shouted. "Lieutenant Crook, are you all right?"

Struggling to stand, dizziness drove Crook to sit back down. Confusion forced his voice into a halting tone, like he was unsure if he was still alive. "Yes, Sergeant...I think am fine...though I fear he stuck me good,"

Searching about, Crook looked at the burning torch lying to the side and the crumpled form of his foe next to it. The Indian wasn't moving.

Crook motioned to his bleeding leg, and Loraine began dressing the wound. Loraine clearly had a lot of practice at it, and he stripped cloth from a pouch to tie around the injury.

"Good thing you moved him up a bit," said Loraine, working quickly with his makeshift bandage. "It was the only way I could manage the shot."

As first aid continued, Crook heard a choking sound. Realizing it was coming from the Native, he scooted over to the fallen brave as Loraine cinched a strip around his wounded leg.

Flipping him over, Crook stared down at the ghastly face of his enemy. The man's jaw was missing, and jagged flesh protruded from the mortal wound.

The Native tried to talk, but only garbled sounds escaped his mangled face. The anger and hatred, so apparent moments ago, was replaced by something different. As the Native choked out gasping sounds, he looked terrified and absolutely human. His scared eyes were desperate and pained from his impending demise.

Crook's own demeanor moved to compassion from the pitiable image. As his foe's choking attempts at breathing wound down, Crook clutched the man's hand in his own. While the Native died, Crook met his gaze with a kind nod.

After the man breathed his last, Crook righted himself and again tried to stand. Swooning, he stumbled and collapsed to one knee. His vision now blurred, he attempted to blink away the opaque nighttime surroundings.

Instead, he fell over, and darkness overtook him.

#

The sun's rays flooded across Crook's face, lighting up his youthful features. Despite his exacting temperament and arduous duties, he could have passed for a much younger man.

Crook's eyelids fluttered open, and he scanned his surroundings, taking in the morning's sights. He lay on a litter attached to his horse, where he was tucked under blankets and animal skins to keep warm from the morning chill.

Around him was a small camp, and his soldiers and the civilian scout were making ready for the trail. Some cleaned up from a meal, while others packed supplies onto their various horses.

Two bodies lay under blankets near the horse where Selby's remains were still strapped, while one vigilant trooper stood guard with his weapon raised toward a distant tree line.

Near the fire pit, a small girl stood near Pugh as he packed up a series of pots. She stepped close to watch as Pugh doused the fire with a splash of dirty water.

Crook recognized her, and his face grew sad with an unspoken thought.

"Lieutenant, how are you feeling?" asked Loraine, interrupting his thoughts and handing him a canteen.

Not immediately responding, Crook took a long swig from the container and continued watching the girl. "Sergeant Loraine, thank you for asking. I...am tired."

Loraine squinted at Crook, trying to determine his health. His obvious concern was touching, and Crook smiled in thanks as he continued his overwatch of the packing activities.

"Understandable, sir. You've lost a great deal of blood. We were worried you would not recover your senses," Loraine said, his voice growing grave. "That Indian was a tough bastard."

Crook nodded in quiet agreement. Motioning to the young girl, he changed the subject. "I see that the Scott daughter is in satisfactory shape. What of her father?"

Stepping closer, Loraine lowered his voice and gestured to one of the covered corpses. "Unfortunately, he was slain by the savage. With her mother gone from fever last winter, she's now alone."

Crook stared at the camp scene, unsure of what to say next. Finally, he sighed, gesturing to the entire property with a reserved frown. "We take her with us, then. When we return to the fort, we shall send some men to fetch the animals from this cursed ranch."

Sitting up as best as he could, Crook motioned to the corral and mostly empty barn. The cows shuffled in their constricted area, waiting to be let out to graze. "There is always a need for fresh beef and horses."

Loraine grimaced and walked over to a dented pot of coffee on a grate covering the campfire. Pouring a cup of the steaming brew, he returned and offered it to Crook.

Smiling, Crook turned down the offer, instead motioning to the bodies. "Sergeant, please ensure that all of the bodies are brought to the fort, including the brave."

Loraine raised his weathered brow in a silent question. In response, Crook smiled humorlessly and fell back into his litter. "His tribe will want the body back, and that could prove useful if we are to discover the reasons behind their depredations."

Nodding, Loraine lifted the coffee and sipped, savoring it with an appreciative grimace. Puzzling over the encounter with the warrior, he stared back to the now-abandoned ranch house. "What has gotten into the Indians? It does them no good to conduct themselves this way. Everything was better for the last year. There's been no need for violence for some time now...I had even hoped..."

As Loraine trailed off in disappointment, Crook agreed to the sentiment with a tilt of his head. Speaking in a considered tone, he let his gaze roam over the surrounding forests, as if he soon expected another of their enemies to emerge.

"I wish I knew the reasons for this violence, Sergeant. I do not yet understand the reasons for the Natives becoming inflamed against us, but I mean to find out—for all our sakes."

Chapter 3

The Officers' quarters were tidy and functional. An attractive painting of George Washington hung on one wall, while two of the others contained a rendition of a breathtaking waterfall, as well as a high-mountain lake surrounded by an ancient crater. Though official-looking, the space was pleasant and neat, evidencing an occupant that kept everything clean and in proper order.

The room also contained a bed, a footlocker, and assorted simple furniture, including a large wardrobe. Everything was wiped clean, and the wood shined from the efforts of being dusted on a consistent basis.

Frustrated, Crook sat straight-backed on his perfectly made bed. Reading a copy of *Moby-Dick*, he tried to focus on the book's small words from the dim light leaking through a spotless window.

Crook's rigid military bearing ruined his attempt at lounging, and he stood up, trying to read while walking back and forth across the wooden floorboards. With a ponderous limp in his wounded limb, it was apparent he hadn't recovered from the fight at the ranch.

Crook paced there for some time, and his scraping boot from his injured leg provided the only sound in the otherwise quiet room. His eyes darted down the book's pages, focusing and refocusing on each paragraph in an attempt to take in the famous tale of Captain Ahab and his pursuit of a white whale.

Not able to absorb the story, Crook shook his head in frustration. He set the book down, where he revealed his perfectionism by aligning its spine precisely to the edge of his polished desk.

Feeling discouraged, Crook raised his voice. "Private Evans."

After some stumbling from outside, the door opened, and Private Evans entered the room. Looking bashful and unsure, Evans appeared young, even in a time when soldiers routinely served in their middle-teens. The wisp of undeveloped beard on his face didn't dispel that too-young impression, and although his uniform was well maintained, it was also too big for his slight frame.

"Lieutenant, you should go easy on your leg. It's only been—"

"Thank you, Private Evans, but I fear I will lose my mind if I wait in these damn quarters any longer," Crook replied, cutting him off.

Evans lowered his eyes and avoided saying more, obviously unhappy at having offended Crook.

Seeing the man browbeaten, Crook lightened his tone and tried to sound more fatherly. "I appreciate the concern, Private. Might I inquire as to when Captain Judah will accept my report in person? It has been a week since our return."

Evans avoided Crook's inquiring stare, finding the clean floor more interesting to watch. "The captain is often busy...and difficult to talk to."

"You mean drunk and of ill temperament?" asked Crook. "One would think he could occasionally manage to perform his duties."

Silence followed the criticism. For some time, they both considered the conversation, and Crook finally sighed, striking a conciliatory tone as he ventured a grin at the bashful soldier

"All right, Private, there's no need to announce me at this point. I will make a report in person to the captain."

Evans was relieved at the opportunity to avoid conflict and promptly grinned back at Crook. After a sharp salute, he exited the room.

Crook walked to a mirror on the wardrobe. Wetting his fingers, he smoothed out his beard and mustache, ensuring perfect whisker harmony in his reflection.

Considering something, Crook looked back to some papers on his desk. Taking up a quill, he dipped it into an inkwell. Writing for several minutes, he periodically re-dipped the quill and added to the flourishing calligraphy on the paper.

Finally, he signed the paper with an easily readable *George R. Crook*, and when done, he nodded his approval and also aligned that paper with the desk's edge.

Putting on his ironed and brushed officer's coat, Crook limped from the room.

Outside, the fort was small but well laid out. Surrounded on all sides by a twelve-foot fence, the military post housed several buildings as barracks, along with stables, supply buildings, and a few structures for officers and visitors.

The grounds were well manicured, and stones were placed in lines to outline the perimeters of the main common areas. Numerous soldiers performed duties in the background, while others drilled on an expansive parade area near the entrance to the fort.

Crook looked across the post to a distant, centrally located building. In front of the structure was a flagpole flying the American flag, and a soldier stood guard to the side of its entrance. Crook walked toward it, making his way in jerking strides.

Clanking from a blacksmith's shop near his path accompanied Crook's awkward stroll across the open grounds. He passed two soldiers walking patrol with muskets raised and returned the salutes of two more troopers as he got close to the headquarters building.

Nodding to the sentry, he rapped on the door.

From inside, a voice proclaimed, "Enter."

Pacing into the commander's room, Crook snapped a perfunctory salute to Captain Judah, who sat behind a cluttered desk. The commander, in his forties and balding, was perched on his chair in a slovenly manner. Completing his improper military image, he was unshaven and dressed in a messy uniform.

Around Judah, the office was largely nondescript, with basic furniture and several old maps hanging on the walls.

Except, on one wall, a painted portrait of a beautiful woman with long blonde hair and green eyes looked down at the military men.

Scraggly and disinterested, the captain ignored the salute—and didn't notice when Crook dropped the military gesture without a response.

Judah looked down at piles of papers on his desk, shuffling them around intermittently. Mumbling under his breath, he searched for something specific in the jumble of requisitions and paperwork. Elsewhere on the desk were folders and books, none of which were organized in good order.

A bottle of whiskey and a dirty glass also took up space on the messy desk. The glass was empty, and the bottle was largely drained of its brownish contents.

Looking up, Judah's bloodshot eyes met Crook's. He studied Crook for some time, clearly not liking what he saw. Motioning to the lieutenant with a flourish, he slurred his words out. "Why, Lieutenant Crook, I'm glad to see you. So nice...to see you."

Looking conspiratorial, Judah pointed to his whiskey glass in an offering, but Crook declined with a curt shake of his head.

Unabashed, Judah grabbed the bottle and poured the bottle's final generous portion into his glass.

"I am here to report on our scouting mission and our subsequent return. I submitted a written report already, but—" said Crook, even as Judah held up a finger to silence him.

Judah continued searching amongst his things and was finally able to track down the elusive report. Raising the paper to better see it in the room's deficient light, he focused wryly on Crook. "Ahh, here it is. You've stirred up quite a tempest, haven't you?"

Grabbing his glass, Judah took a full sip of the pungent liquid. His eyes rolled back as he processed the strong alcohol with a contented grunt. More relaxed, he leaned back in his creaking chair.

"And you found our own man, Shelby—"

"Selby, Sir."

"—dead. That is awful."

Pausing, Judah looked up to the portrait on the wall. He stared at the unknown woman for several seconds, losing himself in thought. Suddenly, he returned his gaze back to Crook, and his eyes refocused on the present.

"And you found Mr. Scott dead at his ranch, as well?" Judah asked, continuing his disinterested interrogation.

"Yes, he—"

"Terrible. You engaged and killed a savage there?"

Crook waited a moment before answering, wanting to avoid being cut off again. Breathing deep, he continued in a moderate voice, maintaining his composure as he stared down at Judah.

"I engaged an Indian, and I was saved from certain death by Sergeant Loraine's excellent marksmanship. It's all in the report...sir."

"Yes, so it is."

Stepping closer to the desk, Crook raised his tone, making his words clear and serious. "Sir, there's something that requires our attention regarding the local Indian tribe. They seem to be incensed about—"

Judah chuckled rudely, interrupting Crook. He spread his arms to indicate the area all around them. "They're always incensed about something, Lieutenant Crook. That is why we're in this...lovely place."

"Yes sir, but surely there must be a reason for their violent behavior," said Crook, trying to plead a case for moderation and restraint. "After all, they agreed to peaceful coexistence—"

A derisive snort from Judah.

"—and they have been honest and unthreatening. I have met their chief, Hakan, and he is an honorable man."

Judah snickered and took another sip from his glass. Blinking up at Crook, he was obviously unconvinced by the lieutenant's words and wasn't bashful about showing his skepticism.

Standing with some effort, Judah walked over to the mysterious woman's portrait, stopping to gaze up at her. Wistful and dreamy, he stared at the painting for a considerable time, almost as if he was conversing with it on some inner level.

Crook peered at Judah as if the captain had gone mad. Bewildered, Crook glanced back and forth between Judah and the painting, waiting for some further communication from him. It was an awkward moment, one in which Crook came to the jarring realization that Judah was both a drunk and somehow living in another reality.

After a further moment of interior thought, Judah shook his head and stumbled back to his chair. When he reassumed his doubtful gaze at Crook, he motioned for him to continue.

Taking up where he left off, Crook cleared his throat and tried to appear both confident and reasonable. Inside, he felt neither. "I should like to take a patrol and parley with Hakan. Our mandate is not simply to fight the Natives, but to engage them in a peaceful pursuit."

Emerging from his alcoholic stupor, Judah's face flashed anger. Trying to stand again, Judah thought better of it and dropped back into his chair.

Judah's voice was threatening as he pointed up at Crook. "I am the one who decides what our mandate is here, Lieutenant Crook. I could care less what the Indians think or feel—about anything. You forget your place in this matter."

Crook nodded, keeping his cool. Raising his eyebrows to the drunken officer, he awaited the next words with some reservation.

"We are down to forty men here, with half our troopers being sent to San Francisco," said Judah, motioning to a map on the wall showing the entirety of California. "Because of the damned Civil War."

Smiling like it pained him, Crook kept his voice low. "No disrespect intended, Captain. I am well aware of the happenings in the East. They make our position even more—"

"That is good, because we are going to solve this little local rebellion on our own, with some good old-fashioned punishment," Judah interrupted. "The way it should always have been done before. Our kid-handed treatment of the Indians has precipitated these events. Made them bold and us soft. It is my intention that they will soon feel the bite of our belt on their collective asses."

Judah leaned forward on the desk. His eyes were more aware now, and his voice became clearer. He pounded his fist into the assorted papers, and several sheets fluttered to the floor.

"You are to take eight men and proceed to Hakan's village. You will bring the chief back in shackles, whereupon he will be hanged for the deaths of Shelby and Mr. Scott. Justice will be served on my watch. No more half-measures."

Growing alarmed, Crook was speechless. Exasperated, he lowered his voice—almost to a whisper. "Captain, that would be unwise. The tribe would present a substantial threat—"

"You will heal your leg completely before you depart, so I give you ten days to prepare for the expedition," continued Judah.

Judah pointed an accusing finger at Crook, and his eyes were aggressive, begging for confrontation. "In the meantime, do not send any more of our men on patrol. I will not risk any more of them until this matter is resolved. Until we have stretched the neck of this...Hakan."

Crook considered Judah's commands, mulling over the flagrant stupidity of the proposed action. Crook knew that Hakan had no more control of every Native in the area than Crook himself had over every soldier stationed in the far-flung areas of California or the Oregon Territory. To execute an able leader, someone who had helped them keep the peace in this area for the recent past, was beyond foolhardy—it was positively asinine.

But Crook was also aware he was not completely in charge, and he needed to tread with some caution in matters where he did not decide policy. Judah was a fool, but he was also a fool that could make his life—and the lives of his men—difficult, and that was putting it mildly. Sighing internally, Crook held Judah's gaze for several moments as he decided his next course of action.

Judah continued to glower up, fixing Crook with his awkward grin and partially unfocused eyes. As they measured each other up, the possibility of outright insubordination from the lieutenant touched on both of their thoughts.

Coming to a decision, Crook nodded and saluted, which Judah pointedly returned. Spinning about, Crook exited the building and limped into the late afternoon.

No goodbye was offered or given from either side.

When Crook was gone, Judah cradled his almost-empty drink and kicked his feet onto the desk. Sighing and descending again into his internal thoughts, he resumed his stare at the pretty lady on the wall.

#

Chief Hakan sat cross-legged on a bearskin rug, gently puffing on a long pipe. Around him was the interior of a teepee, with more skins of various other animals covering the walls.

In the middle of the dwelling was a cooking pit, and pots of food were suspended above bright coals underneath. Smoke rose from the pit, causing blurred vision in the interior of the space before exiting the conical vent above.

Across from Hakan sat Silah, who was distressed and emotional. The younger man moved his gaze around the elder Chief, as if not wanting to show disrespect by meeting his eyes directly.

Putting a white root in his mouth, Silah chewed on it to control himself and tamp down his inclination to speak out of turn.

Finally, Silah stared at Hakan expectantly, gently imploring his leader with his features and tone. "Another of the villages is empty, its people gone. If we don't move on the soldiers now, there will be none left to resist them. We must fight like warriors—and not be like pigs set out for slaughter."

Hakan set down his pipe, keeping his eyes aloof and not responding immediately to the young brave. He pondered for a time, running through his options in careful consideration of the consequences for him and his people.

Reaching back, Hakan undid his ponytail, allowing his remarkable streaked hair to fall to his shoulders. His voice was controlled and considerate when he spoke. "And you found dead soldiers in the village? Or something else proving they've moved against us?"

Fidgeting with a necklace of black beads around his neck, Silah became more reserved than before. Avoiding Hakan's inquiring stare, he shook his head. "Not yet, Chief Hakan. They must have carried away their dead or ambushed our people without injury."

"Do you not find it strange that these white men—soldiers, as you say—travel through our lands and hunt our people without a trace? They pass like an owl in the night, with no one to see them?" Hakan asked.

Silence filled the teepee in response. Silah lowered his voice, becoming calmer. "I know that we can't stand by and be destroyed without a fight. The tracks of the white man have been found in many places. What other proof do we need? We are not women, hiding from danger and accepting our fates."

"Tracks of bare feet and our own moccasins have also been found. Do you also think we are being attacked by other tribes? Are there Indians allied with the soldiers at the fort?"

No immediate response came from the youthful Silah. Looking unsure, the fury from his earlier words had died down.

"Do not think that I am careless about our people's lives, young Silah," Hakan said, fixing the brave with an affectionate gaze. "There is a time to fight, a time to kill, and a time to make our enemies tremble from our wrath. But that time is not now. Something is very wrong, and it may be something far worse than the white man."

"What do you mean, Chief Hakan?"

Hakan nodded at the younger warrior, choosing his words carefully. "You know that the wolf hunts in packs? He is the most fierce of hunters, but his strength comes from confusing his prey."

Hakan motioned down to the bear rug he sat on, running his fingers over the dark fur. "Even the mighty brown bear can be slain by the wolf, as they hound him from different directions. When the bear strikes at one of his tormentors, another can attack from behind. In this way, the fierce bear can be overcome, becoming food for the pack."

Silah looked doubtful. "What does this mean for our enemies? Are they circling us, culling the weak from our outlying villages? What do we do to stop them? How do we make them pay for their evil?"

Hakan took up his pipe and puffed again. He considered Silah's questions, blowing rings into the smoky air as he contemplated their fraught relations with the white men.

"We first must find who our enemy is," Hakan said. "When that is done, we can lay a trap—if war is unavoidable. Even a wolf pack can be ambushed and destroyed with the right preparation."

Silah nodded, his enthusiasm growing at the notion of revenge.

"But I warn you, Silah, it may be that our enemy could be something else, something much worse than the soldiers," said Hakan, and he gestured at the wider world outside the teepee entrance.

Silah became puzzled, tilting his head and looking at Hakan. Unsure of the chief's intention, he waited quietly.

"Bring in all our people from the outer villages. Ensure that we only travel in war parties, and not one family is to be left unprotected," said Hakan, sounding serious and committed. "We will set a trap, but I hope that we can manage to kill what we catch. If a clever dog manages to corner a bear, the dog must find a way to survive the fight."

Nodding, Silah peered directly at Hakan, trying to fully understand as he focused on the chief through the whirling smoke.

#

A cascading river flowed down the gorge, splashing in eddies and frothy rapids across time-worn rocks. The tract of water was forbidding, and its raw wildness was sharpened by crashing sounds in the narrow confines of nearby stone and bedrock.

To either side of the river was rough foliage and the sheer walls of a canyon. The sound from the raucous rapids reached all the way to the heights of the cliffs, droning in an eternal and loud chorus. The magnitude of the noise carried far into the distance outside of the ravine.

Farther down the river, the canyon dropped away, and the water drained into a wider and lush background. Trees drooped over the edges of the meandering waterway, and the calmer surface splashed gently against banks of mud and pebbled beaches.

In this area, the mellowing currents turned over into brackish-green hues. An extensive pool stretched across the basin, creating a placid and peaceful surface.

On that calm surface, a disturbance grew. From the dark water, a head rose out of its depths.

Chindi, the possessed Abraham, exited the pool onto the remote beach. Behind him, eight more figures trundled out of the river, including his brother Billy. They were methodical and careful as they walked, appearing in control of their faculties and movements with each purposeful stride of their putrid legs.

Each of these former people was a walking monster, with mottled gray skin and oozing sores over their entire bodies.

Their faces were expressionless, with white, pupil-less eyes and leering, evil gazes. They were not mindless, because within their horrid stares was an abominable intelligence.

The group of nine included seven former Natives, and they all assembled on an open stretch of sand after they exited the river.

Chindi stopped in front of the group and shifted in a circle, sniffing noiselessly. Facing to the northeast, he resumed his march. As one, the group continued behind him, and their waterlogged feet slapped against the dirt-encrusted earth in concert with the unspoken command to move ahead.

As they marched forward, the sounds of birds and nature died away in their path, and the backdrop around them grew silent. Their presence seemed to kill off sound itself, as if nature could not see fit to acknowledge their unnatural existence.

Behind them, the water continued its lazy flow against a natural dam below the point Chindi and his retinue crossed the pool. Against that stone barrier, scores of dead fish collected in the gentle current.

#

Two oil lamps illuminated the room, while minimal sunlight flooded through the window in patches.

Crook sat at his desk writing several names on a blank parchment. He deliberatively considered each name before writing another, taking his time to ensure the choice was appropriate for the job he had in mind.

A sharp knock came to the exterior of his quarters, and Crook's face turned to the door in response. "Who is it?"

Loraine's voice answered from outside. "It's me, Lieutenant, Sergeant Loraine. You requested my presence?"

Setting aside his paper, Crook stood and swung the door inward, allowing Loraine into the tidy room. He met Loraine's gaze with a friendly smile, looking genuinely happy to see him.

Loraine, being a lifetime non-commissioned officer in the army, was unnerved by the kindness and assumed a guarded expression.

Saluting, Loraine focused on Crook with the savvy eyes of one who knew something was amiss. Overt kindness from an officer always meant a unique duty was on offer, wherever and whenever common soldiers served their time.

Crook maintained his smile and motioned for Loraine to sit. "At ease, Sergeant. Can I offer you a drink?"

Loraine nodded and accepted a metal cup of dark liquid. He squinted after taking a sip, his eyes bulging in response to the strength of the harsh spirits. "That's strong, Lieutenant. You could afford better on an officer's pay, I would think."

Crook chuckled and laid the paper he'd been working on in front of Loraine.

Speaking in a kind tone, Crook sat back in his chair. "Loraine, may I call you Lorenzo? We can avoid the formality for now. I...have decided that anyone who endeavors to save my life deserves my complete respect. You are an impressive soldier."

Loraine shrugged, then focused down on the paper. After he finished reading the names, he peered up at Crook, a suspicious look in his expression. "It's just something anyone would've done, Lieutenant."

"That may be the case, Lorenzo, but few could have made that shot with a musket in the darkness, and avoided striking me in the process."

Glancing down, Loraine said nothing more. He was uncomfortable being praised and moved to change the subject. "Why am I here, Lieutenant? It's not Army protocol to drink with subordinates, especially with home-brewed liquor."

Holding his smile, Crook stood and paced the room. His leg still bothered him, but it had improved substantially, allowing him to move easier.

Crook kept his voice pleasant. "I want to tell you about our next mission, and also about the changes I am making to our orders. Changes that are necessitated by our inept commander."

Loraine blinked several times, taking in the information. He raised his disturbed gaze to Crook in response. "Sir?"

Crook laughed, showing a snake-oil-salesman grin, one that implied a sense of camaraderie with the sergeant. "You know that our commander, Captain Judah, is a drunk and a malingerer? That he routinely abuses his office? That he is unworthy to hold command, here or anywhere else?"

Loraine looked away, as if considering whether these were trick questions. "I know that he drinks...perhaps to excess. I also know the penalty for mutiny."

Crook's smile faded away, and he grew serious. He returned to his desk and straightened out his already-organized papers.

Meeting Loraine's equally serious stare, Crook's tone and demeanor became direct. "As do I, Lorenzo. I have spent the entirety of my adult life in the army."

Crook lowered his voice, delivering his words with icy precision. "So, I also know what is moral, and by extension, immoral for a man to do. Captain Judah has issued an immoral order, one that I cannot in good conscience follow."

Loraine was quiet and kept his features guarded, as if considering which side would be best to choose in the suddenly intriguing competition within the officers' ranks.

Showing his skepticism, Loraine extracted a pouch of tobacco from a uniform pocket and stuffed a big wad into his mouth. Keeping his stare noncommittal, he let the chaw percolate in his cheek.

Crook noted Loraine's doubts but pressed ahead. "Captain Judah has ordered me to enter the main village of Chief Hakan, in order that he be arrested and put to death."

Loraine glanced uncomfortably at Crook. "The Indians have killed lately…"

Crook shook his head and raised his voice. "*An* Indian has killed, perhaps more, but we know not from where the order came, as well as the reason. Military service has taught me to be careful about making judgments concerning violence and death, especially when it involves a former enemy."

Reaching down, Crook pulled a sheet of paper from a stack and set it in front of Loraine. On the top of the page was written *General Orders*, followed by numbered list of regulations for the military post. Crook pointed to number 5.

"We are to 'keep the peace in a way suitable for the coexistence of all who live in our area of responsibility,'" said Crook. "And that includes the Indians, Lorenzo."

Loraine thought for a moment, concentrating on the document, but his skepticism persisted. "That's true, Lieutenant, but these kinds of orders have been enforced selectively before—with bad results for the Indians."

Crook nodded, meeting Loraine's gaze in sad agreement. "That is certainly the case, but morals are what one follows when it is one's own chance to act in good conscience. What others do is what they will be judged on. Being right is not dependent on orders, it depends on truth."

"What do you propose instead of seizing the chief?" asked Loraine, and he fixed his gaze on Crook, cutting to the chase and demanding a proper answer.

Crook gestured to the paper with the names written on it, staying quiet for the moment. Loraine again focused on the list and carefully noted each soldier.

"We have a week to prepare, so please gather these men for a journey to see the chief," said Crook. "We are going to get his story and prevent more killing. Something is horribly amiss, and we must get to the bottom of it."

Deep in thought, Loraine let the paper fall on the desk and stood. Walking to the window, he stared out, thinking as he watched the open field of the parade ground.

Turning to Crook, he walked near him and crossed his arms in an intimidating posture.

Crook was surprised at the closeness.

"Lieutenant, as a private I took part in the Mexican Campaign," Loraine said. "After watching my comrades fall to typhus and muskets over a period of months, I was there when we took Mexico City."

Loraine's eyes were uneasy and distant, reliving the experience from fifteen years before. "And I had to bayonet young boys who wrapped themselves in their country's flag."

Loraine let his arms fall to his side. He looked steadfast as he clenched his fists—over and over. Sucking on the tobacco juice in his mouth, he regarded Crook with a cool stare, and his low voice came out in something like a growl.

"In 1855, I fought against the Sioux after the Gratton Massacre, where I lost my brother, a man who never offended anyone in his life. He was ritually dismembered by the savages, and I only got his timepiece back as identification."

Loraine ran one index finger over his knuckles, tracing the outlines of several old scars on his right hand. His eyes and tone were distant as he accessed old and torturous memories. "So, we took our vengeance against the Natives under General Harney at Ash Hollow, where I witnessed grown men butchering women and children. Squaws died defending their young, and nobody batted an eye at our side's despicable actions. You ever seen children killed while their mothers screamed, Lieutenant?"

Sighing and controlling himself, Loraine returned to his seat across from Crook. After glancing again at the list of names and post orders, he stared up at the lieutenant. "So, you will have to forgive me for thinking your notions of absolute right are a load of horseshit. There's only staying alive and protecting our own. Nothing else makes sense to me from where I sit in the military chain of command."

Crook looked surprised at the speech, but he wasn't cowed by the story. Leaning forward, he kept Loraine's firm gaze in his own.

"Fair enough, Lorenzo. What you have seen and done is the same that fighting men have gone through since before the time of Christ. Everything you say is worrisome, especially for those that acted dishonorably, from whatever side they fought. But if you are not persuaded by morals, you can perhaps be persuaded by my logic."

It was Crook's turn to stand, and he moved close to Loraine, who was now surprised in his own right.

"If we start a war with the chief over a misunderstanding, we will be fighting with half our strength against a brutal and effective foe. How many of our men will die in that fight, and how many settlers will get slaughtered like your brother in the resulting chaos?"

Moving over to a cabinet, Crook grabbed an envelope and handed it to Loraine. The envelope had a seal in wax on the outside and was signed with Crook's flowing signature.

"This is my legal affidavit. It lays out the irresponsible actions, drunkenness, and breaches of trust by our commander, far into the past and up to the present. If I should fall, you can refer to it in defending yourself from any military punishment. I have sealed it with my name and signature. If you are to go on this expedition, it can only be on a voluntary basis. My honor compels me to make sure your actions are your own—not forced on you by my own choices in this matter."

There was silence for a time, and Loraine carefully thought through Crook's words. Coming to a decision, he nodded and grabbed the paper and envelope. "I'll get the men ready, Lieutenant. Just make sure we don't spend our men's lives cheaply. They're both of our responsibilities, and I plan to see them survive our time in this hostile land."

Crook nodded in surprised agreement, touched by Loraine's selfless concern for his men. In a world of obsessive attention to self-promotion and self-preservation, it was refreshing to see an example of brotherly concern, especially from a battle-hardened leader.

With that, Loraine nodded and paced out the door, letting it clack shut without another word. The room was again silent as Crook sighed and took up the task of yet more paperwork.

47

Chapter 4

The assembled group of eight soldiers and one scout stood in an extended grassy field. It was almost night, and the troopers were examining their weapons in preparation for the trip ahead.

The clicking of rifled muskets and cap-and-ball revolvers were lonely sounds as the men checked the serviceability and the smooth operation of their fighting tools. As they worked, the young soldiers traded concerned glances, allowing worry to fill their faces at what awaited them in the near future.

Crook walked among the men, and with Loraine standing close, examined their firearms, ensuring their proper condition and function.

Nodding in approval at the weapons and his men, Crook shared a moment of encouragement with each, acknowledging their preparations and professionalism with a supportive smile.

After the inspection, Crook stood in the center of the party and motioned to a map in his hand while conversing with Pugh in hushed tones. Pugh didn't appear happy with the unheard conversation, and he shook his head and moved away from the lieutenant to check on his horse.

While Crook continued to study his map, his subordinates began to make camp, with some unloading gear and water from the horses, while others lit a fire to prepare a meal.

Facing out from the well-organized operation were two sentries, holding their muskets and monitoring the shadowed trees at the edges of the meadow. Their alert eyes scanned back and forth, ready for any threats the incoming night might have offered the expedition.

Yet, most of the troopers weren't confident, despite their calm preparations. Their worried eyes focused on the burgeoning darkness, and trepidation plagued their faces as they mechanically performed their soldierly duties.

Crook noticed the foul mood as he oversaw the quiet preparations. Wanting to control the negative atmosphere, he raised his voice.

"Gentlemen, you are all professional soldiers and of superior fighting stock. Of that, I have no doubt. You have never disappointed me and always acquitted yourselves well in this frontier life. Your service and skills are the envy of every officer in this army."

Crook turned in a circle, meeting the gaze of each of his men. Focusing on every man as an individual, he smiled, letting them know of their shared humanity with an awkward grin.

"But I have met the chief, and he is a man of honor," said Crook, trying to appear confident. "I expect that the reason for our trip will bring a simple explanation for these troubles, and there will be no need for violence. It may well be that the perpetrators of these recent murders were in fact renegades that Hakan himself was in conflict with."

Crook lowered his arms, placing his gloved hands on the hilt of his saber and his officer's revolver. This practiced and cultivated image was meant to instill confidence, in both his men and himself.

"But if the need does arise, I trust you all completely with my life, and you can do the same with me," Crook said, expressing himself truthfully. "We are a family, and we shall take care of one another as such. We must always look to our fellow men-at-arms for support in these difficult times. It is our honor and brotherhood that can persist and overcome any obstacle."

The speech got some heartfelt looks of respect from the assembled men. They traded glances and grinned appreciatively at Crook, and the mood lightened considerably.

The party returned to its duties, and separate clusters of men formed around the fire, seeking warmth and counsel from their companions as they settled down for the night.

Nodding with pleasure at the state of the expedition, Crook took a seat on a nearby stump. Extracting a weathered notebook from an interior pocket, he began writing in his journal with a stubby pencil. Leaning forward to get enough light from the campfire, he scrawled on the grainy paper for some time, going slow to be sure his writing was neat and legible.

"Lieutenant?" said Pvt. Evans, standing sheepishly a few yards away.

Looking up to the private, Crook seemed surprised at the interruption. "Yes, Private?"

Stepping closer to Crook, Evans looked like a scared boy, unsure of what to say. "I was wondering if you could tell me about your first fight? I have never been...I mean, I..."

Crook offered a reassuring smile and motioned for Evans to sit near him. Evans did so, glancing nervously around, as if he was unsure if he should be on such close terms with the lieutenant.

"Of course, Private, where should I start?" asked Crook, looking thoughtful in the shadows of the firelight.

Elsewhere around the fire, sounds of laughter and joking resonated throughout the camp as the soldiers settled in for the night.

"In need of direction as a young man, I had the good fortune of being appointed to the United States Military Academy," Crook said, exploring his memories with a detached gaze and internal consideration of his past. "Being raised on a farm, the worldliness of military structure took time to adjust to, but it was nevertheless welcome."

Crook's distant eyes were contented as he sorted through long-ago events. "Following my graduation, I was posted to California to protect immigrants flooding there as a result of gold fever. It was about a decade ago, and it was a splendid time to be a military man. Often, we were the only law to appeal to, and we had to protect the Natives as much as the miners."

Crook's smile faded a bit, and he returned to the present. "We spent most of our time running down common criminals in those days. Renegade Indians, thieves, rustlers, and such. In a time of lawlessness, we were able to do some good. It felt good to be on the side of law and order, with righteousness as our ally."

Standing, Crook put his journal back into his coat pocket. Smoothing over his immaculate uniform, he stared down at Evans. "The first time I encountered a battle was against a band of Natives, a group that had most cruelly murdered a family on a farm in the Oregon Territory. These outlaws, a cantankerous and wretched group, were not inclined to surrender, and in any case, they were not sorry for their depraved actions."

Crook took time to smooth over his mustache, slipping again into that distant time. "So, they had to be killed after we cornered them in a canyon. Justice and common sense called for such an outcome.

A frown came over Crook's face, and he shook his head as he relived the long-ago events in those lawless outlands where might, not justice, had ruled the day.

Stopping himself, Crook remembered the feel of the interaction with not just groups of settlers and hostile Natives, but also with miners and various competing tribes that shared bitter rivalries dating far into their shared past.

What Crook knew about the time seemed like a lifetime ago, where the reality of strikes for gold conflicted with Indians who had their lives upturned by the massive inflow of subsequent wealth-seekers. From this, he knew that conceptions of "right" were entirely dependent on which side your interests lay.

Whereas an innocent family might be butchered by a drunken Native raiding party, it also was the case that Crook had heard of entire villages razed on the mere suspicion of a cattle theft by a particular tribe. It didn't much matter what the truth was for one group or another, all that mattered was where one's personal interests lay.

Crook had always done his best to deal with each conflict in a fair and judicious manner, but he also knew his desire for even-handed treatment was not always shared by various other parties to a conflict—or indeed his own government.

Coming back to himself, Crook shook away his worries about the past and nodded amicably to Evans. "Unfortunately, they took two of my good men with them on their way to hell. Two men that would likely be living to this day if they had been quick enough with their wits."

Evans gulped, not reassured with the conversation. Dropping his eyes to his hands, he rubbed his knuckles with trembling hands.

Noting the young soldier's worries, Crook continued his kind stare, but he sharpened his words to bring the reality of their situation to the private. "Let this be a lesson to you, Private Evans. You are in the business of the force of arms, which requires the use of practiced violence to achieve a mission. It is an honorable profession, one that I have committed my life to."

Crook leaned very close to Evans now. His face was pleasant in the glow of firelight, but his eyes were rigid, even forceful, as he continued. "But when the time comes to act in battle, do not hesitate, or you may end up like my men from so long ago. It will always be primarily in your own hands if you wish to survive an engagement."

With that, Crook patted Evans on the shoulder and walked to chat with several other men near the fire.

Nodding blankly and feeling out of place, Evans silently watched him go.

#

Crook stood atop a broad ravine, looking warily down at a forest of descending pine trees. The sloping thickets below blocked the view of what lay at the bottom of the gorge, while shrubs and brush lying closer to the top made even nearby visibility difficult.

Surrounding the foliage were the brown dirt slopes of the forest floor, and mounds of pine needles were strewn across most of the shadowed ground.

Proceeding into the dark cover of trees, a simple and narrow trail made its way into the dim patches of timber.

Above, birds from high in the trees chirped in the otherwise bright day, while down in the gorge the unmistakable sound of flowing water resounded off the canyon's narrow walls.

Turning around, Crook strode fitfully back to his group of soldiers. As he approached, the men appeared unhappy with their surroundings, as well as their exposure to possible ambush in this unfamiliar area.

"Mr. Pugh, are you certain this is the best way to the village?" asked Crook.

Pugh shook his head, spitting tobacco. "It ain't something I'm sure of, Lieutenant, because nothing is certain out here."

Creeping carefully, Pugh moved down to the edge of the trees. After scanning the woods, he motioned for Crook to join him.

As Crook approached, Pugh kept his voice low. "Unless you want to announce our arrival by takin' the other route, this is our only way to sneak toward the village."

Crook peered down the forbidding trail, focusing into the shaded and overgrown canopy of woods. His fixed gaze was unflinching as he pondered their course of action. "Fair enough, Mr. Pugh, it is a chance we shall have to take."

Turning, Crook gestured back to Loraine, who nodded and crept forward.

"Sergeant, have the men fix bayonets," commanded Crook. "And ensure they travel light, disregarding the heavier supplies. We need to avoid encumbrance on the way to the village.

Brushing his mustache with his fingers, Crook thought for a moment, then motioned back to the crouching soldiers. "Also, please detail two men to stay with the horses on this ridge line. If there is trouble that is too much for our capabilities, we will be returning quickly. Tell them to stay vigilant."

Crook lowered his voice to a whisper. "And ensure they are quiet as they wait. We are not in friendly territory."

Loraine chuckled without humor. "When have we ever been, Lieutenant?"

Nodding, Crook resumed his gaze into the shadows ahead. His features were more serious now, and his attentive eyes were prepared for the worst.

Loraine moved back and quietly relayed orders to the other soldiers. Crouching and holding their muskets low, all but two of the men moved up behind Crook, staying quiet as they arranged themselves carefully behind him.

Motioning ahead and drawing his revolver, Crook took the lead and descended into the seemingly uninhabited forest.

#

Sunlight illuminated the buildings and fences of the fort, casting long shadows across the interior parade area. A United States flag fluttered from a tall pole in the middle of the broad field, and the open ground around it was flushed with the midday heat.

Several soldiers stood in the late-afternoon sun, sweeping brooms across dirt pathways to make the area presentable. As they worked, there didn't seem to be much difference between the before and after-effects of their labor.

Walking toward the bored soldiers, Corporal Hollis made a circuitous show of inspecting their work. Tall and with an effeminate quality to him, his lanky form appeared out-of-place amidst the sea of the gruff fighting men he supervised.

Hollis stepped close to the detail of soldiers, getting the attention of Private Childs. Neither seemed excited about their work.

"When you're done here, make sure you get that area near the stables," said Hollis, pointing at a distant building. "With Crook gone, I got that drunk bastard breathing down my neck. Never could figure out what officers were exactly good for."

Childs looked up from dusting the dust with his primitive broom, scrunching his face into a sarcastic grin. "It took you this long to figure that out? My momma warned me not to join this goat-rope army, but I guess I had to learn it myself. At least I got you to keep me company."

Chuckling, Hollis smiled and looked toward the main headquarters building. When he saw Judah swagger from the building, his light humor and smile wilted.

Below him, Childs continued his evaluation of their efforts for the afternoon. "Corporal Hollis, I may be a lowly private, but I guess you can tell me the benefits of sweeping dirt off other dirt. It's gotta be a secret to good war fightin' that they teach at the academy."

This got numerous laughs from the other soldiers, threatening the effectiveness of their dirt-sweeping operation. The snickers persisted as Judah took note of the group and paced their way.

"Calm the hell down, he's coming this way," Hollis deadpanned. "If he sees everyone smiling, he'll have us court-martialed for violating regulations."

Keeping his head down, Childs breathed deep between chuckles. "Yeah, regulation 102.8. Thou shalt be a miserable wretch working for idiots when in the enlisted service."

More laughs came from the other men, and Hollis hardened his jaw to keep from smiling. Childs was a smartass, but his insight into the army's hierarchical structure was depressingly accurate.

Walking away from the soldiers and toward the approaching Judah, Hollis's eyes watered at the effort of not laughing.

As Judah ambled closer, Hollis threw him a salute.

Judah returned the formality and looked quizzically over Hollis's shoulder at the various working troopers. Crouching low, the men were giggling uncontrollably and avoiding meeting the captain's gaze.

Judah's eyes were red and bloodshot, so focusing on the soldiers was difficult.

"I would presume the duties are being carried out in a satisfactory manner?" asked Judah.

"Yes, sir," replied Hollis, holding back a smile with herculean effort.

"That's good, because I discovered by messenger that an old academy classmate of mine, Lieutenant Gardiner, will be arriving soon with reinforcements. We will be fortunate for the extra manpower."

Still fighting the urge to laugh, Hollis merely nodded.

Judah slipped into his memories, speaking slowly. "I taught Gardiner everything about war fighting I learned at the academy. Only in such a hallowed institution can one learn about the rigors of frontier life and subsequently put such learning into action."

Looking at Judah's stained uniform and matted, unkempt hair, Hollis' features seemed about to explode. After several calming breaths, he muttered quietly. "Yes...sir."

"So, please have the men continue their chores, and make sure to collect those pebbles by the stables. We can't have those getting in the way. We must showcase our fort to be an efficient and clean outpost for our upcoming guests."

Several more controlled breaths by Hollis followed. "Yes...sir."

Nodding affably, Judah gestured behind Hollis to the cleaning soldiers. He appeared concerned at the working soldiers' state of mind. "And corporal, it looks to me as if some of the men are crying. Please ensure they get some rest. Ours is not an army where we mandate our men to be miserable."

Shooting Judah another salute, Hollis nodded and spun back to his men. As he paced to the work detail, a tear of restrained humor finally rolled down his still-clenched jaw.

#

Crook crouched low in front of a substantial creek. Set at the bottom of the canyon, the water trickled in pools and flowed gently across gravel and smooth rocks. Leafy trees hung over the rippling current in both directions from where Crook waited.

Ahead, the waterway wasn't deep and crossing it appeared to be an easy proposition. Crook moved his eyes up the opposite canyon, searching for prospective dangers as he evaluated the group's path going forward.

Behind Crook, his men were spread out and stooped low. They made no sound as they impatiently waited for his orders to move; each man was hypervigilant and leery of their precarious location in the open.

Insects zoomed in circles around the water of the creek's calm pools, and a trout surfaced to the side in pursuit of one of the buzzing morsels.

Farther up the canyon, a chattering of a distant bird also filled the air, sounding like a nagging partner in the high treetops of the canyon.

Nodding to Pugh, Crook motioned ahead to the shallow rapids. The scout stepped quietly forward, ready to cross the open water and find cover on the other side of the trickling creek.

As Pugh waded into the rapids, a whistle came from the last man in the group at the back of the party. Pointing, an excited Pvt. Trumain gestured to a stand of trees on the upstream side of the party.

Barely visible in branches hanging over the tree-crowded shore was a dark figure. The shaded man didn't move as he stood still in the dark undergrowth, and if not for his very specific human outline, he could have been mistaken for a strange bush or trunk.

Reacting quickly, Evans leveled his musket at the shadow, balancing his weapon against the tree for a better aim at their prospective opponent.

Crook followed Evans' lead, raising his revolver and cocking it as he shouted. "If you move, I will be forced to shoot."

A flitting sound came from behind, and Evans cried out, an arrow shaft buried in his shoulder. Surprised, he discharged his weapon into the trees and grabbed at the wound.

"Deploy to skirmish, we're under attack," shouted Loraine, and he, Pvt. O'Rourke, and Pvt. Blenchley scanned the trees behind them for the source of the arrow.

"There," exclaimed Loraine, and he traversed his musket to the side, aiming at a man holding a bow amongst the trees on the hill.

Three booms from their muskets followed, as Loraine and the others fired up the embankment. The bowman showed no reaction, apparently uninjured by the fusillade.

"Charge," shouted Loraine, and the three soldiers scrambled up the slope to close with their adversary.

Aiming carefully, Crook fired his revolver at the still-unmoving figure near the creek but was shocked when it didn't react. Confused, Crook held up his sidearm to inspect it for a misfire.

Speaking over his shoulder, Crook barked in a frustrated voice. "Cover our right flank, Mr. Pugh."

Pugh and O'Rourke faced the opposite direction, holding out their weapons and scanning for further threats.

The figure opposite Crook and Evans stepped from the shadows.

Its face was a living nightmare. It looked to be Native, but it was in no way human, even as it held up a bloody spear in its ugly gray hands. With white eyes and a leering, demonic gaze, it focused and advanced on the moaning Evans.

Crook quick-fired several times, fanning his revolver to increase the speed of his shots. A cloud of smoke blocked the view of the incoming demon, and as his weapon clicked empty, he struggled to see past the haze.

With rushed motions, Crook's shaking hand grabbed a paper cartridge from his pouch and jammed it into one of the smoking-cylinder chambers. Time seemed to stand still as he hurried to complete the reload.

Abruptly, the Indian demon emerged from the hazy smoke, lunging forward at Evans. On its bare chest were now several jagged bullet holes that leaked black fluid down its grotesque bare skin.

Frightened and in agony, Evans backed up, trying to hold the demon off with his musket held in his one good arm. With little control of his shoulder's spasming muscles, his defensive efforts were ponderous and erratic.

Behind Crook, Pugh and O'Rourke fired off several shots as another malignant Native ran from behind a tree and leapt into the air. The fetid brave swung a tomahawk down on Pugh, severing his ear and cutting into his collarbone as he fell on top of the startled scout.

Pugh screamed in agony, trying to push the possessed Native off as he crumpled backward.

Struggling to disengage from his attacker, Pugh bellowed a frantic plea for help. "Get 'em off me."

A panicked O'Rourke ran behind the demon, ramming his bayonet into it over and over. The sharp point barely penetrated the attacker, as the fiend's skin was like rubber over cold meat.

The demonic Native leaned over Pugh, bending down as if to kiss the man. Pugh's eyes were terrified, and he tried to pull away from the horrid aggressor, arching his face to the side.

On the hill above, Trumain was the first to reach the bow-wielding Native. Fetid and gray, this man was also a monster. It had three large holes in its chest from the soldiers' prior blasts but appeared unbothered by the grave wounds. Dropping its bow, the bowman pulled a knife and faced him.

Trumain bayoneted the creature with practiced ease, ramming the sturdy tip of his sharp blade into the stomach of the putrid Indian.

In response, the Native seemed unaffected by the grievous wound to its abdomen. Unconcerned, the devil pulled itself down his rifle, trying to reach Trumain—even as it impaled itself further. As it got closer, Trumain pulled back, horrified and unsure of what to do.

Rushing up, Loraine stabbed his bayonet into the creature's face. Pushing the head to the side, the pointed blade peeled off a large strip of soggy flesh, and black, jellylike gore oozed from the evil Native's dark skin.

Stopping short of the melee, Blenchley watched the unfolding fight with burgeoning horror. Staring blankly at Loraine, he looked around, searching for a path to run away.

Loraine noticed the pending retreat of Blenchley. Flipping his rifle around, he shouted to the fearful trooper. "Club the wretched thing."

Loraine slammed the rifle stock-first into the back of the demon's head. Stumbling from the jarring impact, the filthy foe tumbled over, pulling the impaling rifle from Trumain's hands as it fell.

With the monster on the ground, Blenchley came to his senses and rushed forward. Joining Loraine, they maniacally bashed the Native as it struggled to rise. Their stocks cracked continuously into its misshapen skull, turning its hideous features into a mushy pulp with each energetic swing.

Searching around, Trumain grabbed a huge rock from the ground. Running up, he swung the jagged stone over his head, joining his comrades in bludgeoning the demon. Blood and brain matter splattered the ground as the soldiers pummeled their wicked enemy with continuous bashes of their blunt weapons.

Below with Pugh and O'Rourke, a new sound entered the battle, a hideous one that that assaulted the ears of all present.

It was the sound of inhuman wails, with a rising, crowd-like crescendo laced throughout an audible nightmare. These were screams laced together in a demonic chorus, and they came from the mouth of the Native sprawled on top of Pugh.

His attacker leaned down over Pugh's open mouth, and the otherworldly cascade of dreadful cries poured into Pugh from its black lips. Pugh tried to shriek against the repulsive onslaught, but no sound emerged to fight the auditory invasion. The scout's terrified and tormented eyes moved around, searching for relief from the infernal agony of the otherworldly assault.

No relief came from the sickening onslaught, and Pugh's gaze drifted off to a detached and oblivious stare.

Behind the demon, O'Rourke gave up stabbing the Native. Moving to its side, he rammed the .58 caliber musket toward its ear, and the bayonet carved a channel of blood in its spongy cheek.

O'Rourke pulled the trigger, and the demon's head exploded with a cacophonous crack. The loathsome creature tumbled over, destroyed and unmoving, and the grisly remnants of the Native's head seeped into the moist earth of the creek's bank.

In front of Crook, the spear-armed demon lunged at Evans, who awkwardly parried the creature's thrusts with his rifle bayonet. Circling Evans, the creature moved with intelligence and speed as it sought an opening to pounce on the overmatched soldier.

To the side, Crook finished reloading his pistol and blasted more shots at the hideous assailant. His bullets blew holes in the monster's chest, shoulder, and neck. One bullet blew off the jaw, and black, ragged flesh leaked gore from the wound.

But the Native didn't seem to notice, still focusing on Evans. With a sudden rush, it batted aside Evans's rifle and plunged its spear into the flailing teen's chest. Pressing him back against a tree, the demon pinned him against the bark, and Evans screamed in agony.

"No," yelled Crook, and he dropped his revolver and drew his officer's saber in a rush.

Moving up behind the attacker, he hacked across the shoulders and legs of the creature—but all to little effect. Only small cuts were visible on the tough skin of the revolting monster.

Frustrated, Crook used both hands, rearing back for a forceful blow. His next cut was on the neck of the demon, and it had some affect, biting into its inhumanly tough and sturdy flesh.

Again and again Crook reared back, slicing into the same area on the Native with each successive bite of his thin sword. After a series of blows, his blade cut halfway into the neck.

The monster abruptly fell to his knees, and with sweat emerging across his fierce face, Crook continued his ferocious slashes into the hideous skin.

With a final, desperate hack, Crook decapitated the demonic brave. Still for a moment, the creature's body tumbled over.

But Evans was still pinned against the tree.

Crook rushed to him, gently touching the protruding shaft in his chest. Rendered speechless, the lieutenant cast his glance about, as if searching to find something that could fix the horrible injury.

Instead, Evans reached out and touched Crook's arm. He looked at Crook with the same innocent face, pleading for Crook to make everything right with his boyish features.

"It doesn't hurt too much," said Evans. Just a minute, and I'll be...okay."

Crook's frightened eyes met Evans', and the young trooper smiled through his bloody teeth. At last, he seemed less like a boy and more like a trusted comrade-in-arms. Having stood up to his fears, he had fought bravely at Crook's side.

With a guttural choking sound, the light left Evans' eyes. Slumping to the side, he died.

Sadness flooded through Crook, and he gently pulled the spear out and lowered Evans to the ground.

Crouching over the young man, Crook straightened out the bloodied body, making his repose appear like he was just sleeping. Focusing down, Crook mourned the young man.

After a moment of silence, Crook glanced over at the abomination that killed the boy. Growing exasperated, he stared at the dead-looking flesh of the headless attacker. "What demon in hell?"

From near the creek, O'Rourke called over to Crook. "Lieutenant, it's Pugh."

Stumbling up, Crook hurried over to O'Rourke, who was hunched over Pugh. Motioning to the fallen scout, O'Rourke was panicked and overwhelmed.

Pugh lay on his back and still breathed, despite the blood and muck that covered his face and uniform. The tomahawk was still buried in his shoulder, but his face looked...strange.

With some suddenness, the off-white color of his complexion darkened, becoming gray and sickening in a matter of a few seconds. His pupils began to fade into an all-white background, one they had just witnessed from their demonic opponents.

"Lieutenant," said O'Rourke, growing alarmed and stepping back from Pugh. "There's something wrong..."

The point of Crook's saber plunged deep into one of Pugh's changing eyes. Rearing back, Crook continued ramming his blade into his friend's face, stabbing down until it was soon hacked apart and unrecognizable. Breathing hard, he finished the effort by slicing off Pugh's head, which rolled several feet away.

Behind Crook, Loraine, Blenchley, and Trumain walked up. They each carried bloody muskets and were covered in the creature's gory remnants from up the hill.

It became silent as each of the soldiers peered at Crook holding his blade, and then over to Pugh's decapitated corpse. Nobody appeared willing or able to talk as they took in the horrific scene.

Shaking his head, Crook came to his senses, blinking away his disbelief at the savage violence. "We seem to have encountered something from hell itself."

In response, his men nodded, flashing brief eye contact with each other as they absorbed the extent of the violence and their traumatic losses.

Loraine held up his musket, examining the damaged stock of his weapon. "Whatever they are, they can be killed. Just took a bit of effort."

Crook nodded. Looking back to Evans, he strode over and retrieved his revolver from its place near the body of the demon. After returning to the survivors, he began reloading it.

"Sergeant Loraine, please retrieve the weapons of Private Evans and Mr. Pugh," said Crook. "If your own arms are in disrepair, discard them; we will need to move quickly."

"Where are we goin', Lieutenant?" asked O'Rourke. "We need to—."

"Lieutenant," exclaimed Loraine, pointing up the canyon they had hiked down earlier.

From some distance up the small trail they recently descended, standing under numerous trees, stood Chindi. Chindi watched the soldiers, gently swaying in the shade of several large branches.

Crook squinted into the afternoon light, trying to get a better look at their horrid observer. Frustrated, he went to Pugh's body and retrieved binoculars from one of his carrying pouches. Moving to get a better view, he focused through them.

Chindi was more visible now, but Crook still couldn't make out his precise features. After a moment, Billy moved from the shadows and stood next to his demonic brother, taking his place as the righthand creature of his abominable leader. Neither moved or made a sound—they just watched.

Crook lowered his gaze and handed the binoculars to Loraine. In turn, each of the men used them, peering up at their silent onlookers.

"Wh-what...who is that, Lieutenant?" asked Blenchley.

Shaking his head, Crook continued loading his pistol. When he finished, he spun the cylinder and checked its function. Putting it away, he glanced at each of his men.

"I do not know, and I don't wish to make their acquaintance, either," Crook said. "We must make haste from this place and get to the village. The rules as we have known them on this mission have decidedly changed."

Blenchley was skeptical. "Are you sure that's a good idea, Lieuten…" Blenchley's voice cracked, and he trailed off as he looked first at Pugh, then over to Evans.

Bending down, Crook retrieved Pugh's revolver, wiping blood off it in the process. Walking up to Blenchley, Crook put his hand on the trooper's shoulder and held out the revolver butt-first.

Crook's voice was firm but empathetic as he pointed up to the trees where Chindi stood. "I understand your position, Private, but I also understand something from years of conflict. They are waiting to ambush and finish us off."

After Blenchley haltingly took the weapon, Crook began emptying his pockets and pouches, throwing anything heavy to the ground.

"And we are not going to accommodate them. Please, we leave forthwith," said Crook. "I don't know how long the devils will wait to move on us."

Loraine stepped close to Crook, and he addressed Crook with some severity. "What about Pugh and Evans? Are we leaving 'em for the buzzards?"

Stopping his preparations, Crook maintained his bearing, then offered Loraine a reluctant frown as he spoke. "I should hope that we can come back for them, Sergeant, but the truth is neither one of those superb men would want us to die in order that they be buried. They are, in any case, with God at this point."

Loraine spat to the side, not happy with the answer. Scowling at the other men, he motioned impatiently for them to get ready to depart.

The other soldiers began moving about, dropping extra supplies and taking the knives and guns from the dead. As they formed up, Crook looked at Loraine, offering him a mirthless and forced smile.

"Are you ready, Sergeant?" asked Crook.

Nodding, Loraine spat tobacco to the side, where it landed with perfect aim on the grisly remnants of the fiend that killed Pugh.

"Never was one to overstay my welcome, Lieutenant."

#

The forest was bright and attractive at this time of afternoon. The sun spread bright patches of lights across the shady pine trees, making their needles come alive as a modest breeze ruffled the branches. Through the heights of the canopied woods, birds sang a pleasant melody of staccato chirps.

Pvt. Thompson, young and dark-haired, stared around at the surrounding forest, a sour grimace crossing his face. Frowning, his dour demeanor appeared to be a permanent aspect of his ornery face. "I could've gone anywhere, and I get sent to this godforsaken wasteland. I heard they got entire towns we could've been stationed in out in the Oregon Territory."

Sitting on a stump near the horses, Private Cooper rolled his eyes. Older and a with a sarcastic expression, his tone was skeptical. "You realize that whole regiments of guys like us are getting wiped out in the war back East? My cousin sent me a letter; he said they got piles of corpses in every battle. Said at Antietam they gotta stack the limbs of guys across the fields. They gotta cut off the arms and legs to try to save 'em. Said they die of sepsis otherwise. Maybe we ought to count our good luck?"

Thompson's sour look didn't change, but he conceded the point with a nod. "Yeah, that don't sound too nice. I just wish they had some girls out here. Gets a little lonely staring at deer all day."

Cooper nodded agreement, a playful smirk filling his expression. "Yeah, I was talking to—" Cooper said, and then he stopped abruptly.

Standing up, Cooper cocked his head, searching the tree line. He motioned for Thompson to be quiet.

"What is it?" asked Thompson.

"I dunno. Somethin' ain't right."

Cooper went over to a horse, drawing a carbine musket from his saddle scabbard. Readying the weapon, he held it up and scoured the woods.

Following Cooper's lead, Thompson put a hand on his holstered revolver and scanned in a circle. His surly expression was replaced with confusion.

Cooper nodded, suddenly understanding the problem. "It's the birds. They ain't chirping anymore."

Silence came from all around as the soldiers considered their situation. Then, from the canyon came a distant crack of gunfire.

"Was that a shot?" asked Thompson.

"Could've been...yeah, I think so," replied Cooper.

Three more distant booms echoed from the ravine below them.

"Those definitely were," said Cooper, and he hurried toward the horses. "We better get the horses ready. We might not have any time if they're in a hurry when they get back."

Thompson joined Cooper in preparing the horses for travel, and several more shots emanated from the canyon. After packing up their food and water, they untied the animals and walked swiftly toward the trailhead.

Moving slowly in front, Cooper held his musket up, ready for trouble. Behind him, Thompson walked with several lead ropes of the horses in each hand. Both men were cautious and worried.

Behind, the snap of a twig. Thompson spun around, eyes wide.

Standing between the scattered trees was the familiar form of Lt. Gardiner from Fort Bidwell. His body was outlined in the shaded forest, and to either side of him were four quiet soldiers.

Thompson smiled broadly, ecstatic with the good luck to receive reinforcements at such an opportune time. Wrapping the horses' ropes around a small tree, he stepped toward the group. He grinned broadly, wanting to hug the new soldiers.

Cooper was also happy at the turn of events, and he raised his voice in overt gratitude. "Lieutenant, it's good to see you."

Except, the Lieutenant and his men seemed to move...strangely. None of them returned Cooper's or Thompson's enthusiasm.

Stopping, Thompson grew suspicious. Despite the incoming help, he drew his revolver, holding it down discreetly.

"Lieutenant, how did you come here? Where are your horses? Why aren't ya saying anything?" asked Thompson, his voicing growing shrill.

Gardiner stepped forward without speech or welcome. Moving across a patch of sun, his face became visible.

Gardiner and his men were uninterested in making conversation. With white eyes and dark skin, there was little to discuss as they began sprinting toward the young privates. Their looping runs were not terribly rapid, but they closed the distance fast as they moved with outstretched arms and eager, blank eyes.

From above the broad forest, shots and screams rang through the isolated woods. After a pause, a distant chorus of hellish screams resounded through the woods—the wails of invading fiends, taking new souls.

Breaking their silence, a flock of freshly disturbed birds took flight from the treetops and fluttered into the waning light of day.

#

Night approached, causing the taller grass and brush to appear as dark spots across the extended prairie.

The gloomy Native village was laid out in rows of teepees, with fire pits located at intervals throughout. Surrounded by grassy meadows, the encampment provided clear views of any who would approach it from the outside.

Across one of the fields to its side, Crook's party watched the quiet village. Each man was crouched and silent as they exchanged distressed glances, not knowing what to expect.

In the murky evening, Crook rested on one knee, peering through Pugh's binoculars at the distant conical structures. Loraine was at his side, also crouching and watching intently ahead.

Lowering the field glasses, Crook squinted into the fading light. Doubt clouded his eyes, and he shook his head while gesturing to the tidy rows of teepees. "I cannot see anyone; it looks quiet."

"That doesn't mean anything, Lieutenant, they know what they're doing," Loraine replied. "They can hide in a few blades of grass, and you never know they're here—till it's too late."

"Perhaps, Sergeant, but it is doubtful they would let us get this close to their families. They are a fiercely protective people."

Trumain cleared his throat, trying to be respectful from the back. Turning, Crook looked surprised but nodded for him to continue.

"You remember the time we found that Paiute raiding party all chopped up near the high desert?" Trumain asked. "They were in open ground, and they were skilled warriors. They never saw the end coming, so we best be careful."

Crook lowered his eyes, thinking over their options. "That is true, Private, but in that case their enemies meant them harm. In our own condition, we are not here in that capacity."

Collecting himself, Crook glanced back to the tree line leading to the creek. Gesturing there with a wave of his arm, he spoke in a worried tone. "Additionally, we have bigger concerns from where we just came."

With that, Crook stood and strode into the field. He held his arms away from his weapons, showing peaceful intent as he moved over the open ground.

His men behind reacted with hesitation, then following him one by one while also holding their arms aloft. Under the barely lit sky, the party trudged across the grassland toward the outskirts of Hakan's village.

Nothing occurred as the group strode ahead. No movement or shout of alarm greeted them, and the lack of reaction from inside the village was unnerving.

As they got close to the first huts, everything was quiet. Crook stopped at the edge of the first structure and waited for a sign they had been noticed. When none came, he resumed his normal posture and pointed down a line of silent huts at a specific teepee.

"When I met Hakan in the spring, it was there. He was respectful and an excellent host," Crook said, his voice low and hopeful. "He even allowed himself a few jokes at my expense. We can only hope he retains that demeanor."

Stepping out of cover, Crook walked toward Hakan's teepee, panning his head to either side as he approached. As his men quietly followed, Crook motioned for them to spread out and take defensive positions.

At the entrance, there was light emerging around the edges of the leather curtain. Licking his lips, Crook nudged the curtain aside, preparing for the worst as he stepped inside.

Hakan sat across from the opening, a calm and serious scowl on his face. Around him were numerous stretched animal skins, as well as Native clothing hung on lines.

With a subdued fire burning in front of the chief, Hakan nodded at Crook and motioned to a bright blanket on the floor opposite him. "Crook, you are here at last. Please, sit."

Crook stopped, taking in the scene and considering the situation. Nodding, he moved to the indicated spot, where he awkwardly took his place facing Hakan.

They stared at one another for a while, each taking a measure of the other's circumstance and intentions.

Breathing deep, Crook motioned around them to the uninhabited village. "Where are your people, Chief Hakan?"

Hakan motioned to the west, keeping his face rigid. "I sent them away, Crook. There is much danger for my people if they stay."

The chief didn't elaborate further, as if such an event was a normal way of living. He waited for Crook to speak.

Crook nodded, as if agreeing with the sentiment. Irony filled his voice as he raised his tone. "There is danger for any that inhabit this area, Chief. Even for the ranchers and soldiers you swore to leave in peace."

"This is why you come to me, Crook?"

Crook sighed, shaking his head and fixing his intense gaze on the chief. "I have come on the orders of my commander, Captain Judah. He is most displeased that your braves have killed innocent men. Your explicit guarantees from our earlier meeting indicated that such events would be a thing of the past."

Hakan frowned and nodded, showing his discomfort with the subject. He was not confrontational, but neither was he intimidated. "This is true, Crook, and not good. There is bad reason for this."

"I am listening, Chief."

Hakan motioned around them—toward the wider world. "There is great evil that comes to this area. An evil one—you call him demon—has made this area cursed. He comes to avenge himself on all humans living here."

Leaning forward, Crook acknowledged the chief's words with a tilt of his head. Focusing on the Indian leader, he spoke coolly. "We have fought something like you describe on the way to your village. Is this what happened to make your people kill? Or, to make them flee?"

"Some young braves attacked because they thought the white man was taking our people. Villages were becoming empty," replied Hakan, and his tone was apologetic. "And now they leave to avoid this demon. Other tribes to the west take them in...so we can avoid this enemy together."

"But you are still here? What can you do alone?"

Hakan didn't answer as he stared into the fire. Reaching down, the chief rubbed the end of his long smoking pipe as he considered what to say next.

"Chief, what is happening in this country? What is the source of this pestilence?" asked Crook, clearly baffled.

From the front of the teepee, a soft tap came from the stretched-skin barrier, followed by Loraine's heavy voice. "Lieutenant, we found an Indian woman in the village. She says she's the chief's daughter."

Loraine pushed the flap aside to reveal a thin woman at the barrier. Nayeli, pretty and young, stood in the dim light and glared inside.

Hakan rose quickly and strode to the entrance. He fixed her with a fierce gaze, and his disapproval at her presence was obvious.

Nayeli stared back at her father, as proud and unrumpled as she was beautiful. She moved inside the teepee, ignoring Hakan's reproving stare as she remained standing.

Crook peered up at Nayeli, unable to hide his enchantment at the young woman's looks. He was a methodical man with an almost inhuman capacity for self-control, but even he could not ignore the presence of such an attractive woman at the edge of the settled world. In response, Nayeli noticed his interest but remained focused on her father.

"Crook, this is my daughter," said Hakan. "Her name is Nayeli. She doesn't listen to me."

Despite the serious events, Crook couldn't avoid smiling.

Nayeli raised a defiant tone to her father. "I will not leave my father here to fight Chindi alone. He can't face devil without help from his people."

"Chindi?" asked Crook.

Sighing, Hakan looked from Nayeli to Crook and back again. Considering his words carefully, he spoke plainly. "This is what cause the demon problem, Crook. Chindi is here to destroy people from all tribes, including white man."

Standing up, Hakan looked around carefully. Straightening his tunic, he walked to the back of the teepee and began packing supplies into several satchels.

Crook and Nayeli both looked at him, baffled as to what he was doing.

"Father, what...?" asked Nayeli.

"We will travel to fort, where we tell captain about this problem," Hakan replied, and he stuffed the bags with foodstuffs for the trip. "I tell everything on way to fort."

Exasperated, Crook rose to his feet. "Chief Hakan, that would be unwise. If you return to the fort, you could be imprisoned and hung by the captain. We should think of somewhere else to plan the next move."

Nayeli nodded agreement, suddenly appearing more worried and less courageous. She implored her father with her tone. "Yes, Father, we must prepare for Chindi away from soldiers. They will take revenge on you for our warriors' bad actions."

Finishing his packing, Hakan shook his head. Stubborn, he spoke in a voice not intent on compromise. "No. If we wait here, we will be destroyed by devil Chindi. If we do not visit Captain, all will die, and no one can live in this land. Everything will be lost."

Brusquely, Hakan barged out the door, leaving Crook and Nayeli to gaze at each other in his wake. Their stares continued for some time, and Crook grudgingly tore his eyes away from Nayeli.

Blushing, Crook raised his voice. "Sergeant Loraine, please make ready to travel, immediately. We will be returning to the fort as soon as possible, and the chief and his daughter will accompany us."

"Will do, Lieutenant," replied Loraine from the darkness.

Outside, there were immediate sounds of movement as the soldiers complied with the order. Crook's eyes lingered on Nayeli as he looked for something to say.

"I...umm...pray your father knows what he is doing," Crook said.

After trading a last glance with Crook, Nayeli nodded shyly. Hesitating, she appeared inclined to talk, but after a few moments, shook her head and exited the teepee.

Alone in the chief's quarters, Crook felt flustered, a sensation he was not accustomed to. Still embarrassed but unsure of the reason why, he sighed and followed her out.

Chapter 5

Pale moonlight barely lit the remote trail, making it strangely fluorescent against a dark backdrop of scattered trees and shrubs.

Loraine stared down the trail, uncertain and worried. Turning, he crept back to the rest of the party, who crouched near some bushes in the dim scenery.

"Pugh was better at this, but I think it's clear," said Loraine. "It should be safe to make camp if we don't light any fires."

Leaning down, Crook eyed each member of the party. Staring at Hakan for confirmation, he motioned to the side of the path.

"Gentlemen, we shall rest here for the night," whispered Crook. "Eat quickly and get some sleep. We may not have sufficient time later to rest. We leave at first light."

As the party spread into the brush to the side of the trail, the group moved carefully and spoke in hushed tones.

Hakan and his daughter found a place to sit on raised boulders to the side, where they watched the camp take form as the soldiers moved about in silence. Taking out a pouch of seeds, Hakan shared them with Nayeli, and they thoughtfully chewed in silence.

After some time, Crook approached the duo.

Nodding at the lieutenant, Hakan motioned for Crook to talk, and Crook accepted the invitation by lowering himself opposite them.

Getting to the point, Crook was not bashful about wanting more information. "I would like to hear more about your story, Chief."

In response, Hakan looked to his daughter, pleading with his eyes for her to move away and allow them to speak privately. Nayeli duly ignored her father and gestured for the conversation to move on.

Sighing at his stubborn offspring, Hakan shook his head in frustration. When he spoke, he kept his voice low. "What do you want to know, Crook? You said you fought Chindi already?"

"We fought creatures that seemed to be spawned from hell, Chief, and they were difficult to kill," replied Crook. "They looked to be dead in appearance yet moved fast and without weakness. They were not harmed by weapons in the way of normal flesh."

Hakan acknowledged Crook's experience with a tilt of his head, but he remained reluctant to respond, as if it was too much to expect Crook to understand.

Frustrated, Crook leaned close to Hakan, allowing a hint of demand to enter his tone. "Be so kind as to tell me about this 'Chindi.'"

Grinding his jaw, Hakan motioned to the remote area around them that made up his tribe's homeland. "It is evil spirit that is from dead man...a man from long ago, when the land was not controlled by the white man. This demon is from world of Indian, but now it takes form of a white devil."

Confused, Crook stared, not registering what the chief meant.

Hakan noticed his bewilderment. "When man dies, his spirit leave body. But when evil man dies, his spirit can remain."

Looking around, Hakan sought a prop to explain what he meant. Pointing to Crook's pack on the ground, he continued. "And spirit can be trapped in something evil man used in life, like your pack."

Crook was skeptical, and he peered first at Hakan, then his daughter. His doubt wasn't lost on the pair.

"Your belief is not necessary, Crook. Chindi is here and wants to control all our land and kill the people. Can you not believe your eyes?" asked Nayeli.

Looking perplexed, Crook acknowledged the obvious. "Well, something horrible is certainly occurring."

Hakan continued his explanation. "Evil spirit can take the body of weak man and spread. Chindi can bring new demons to new men. He multiplies, like rabbit in a field without predators."

Hakan looked into the night sky, taking in the innumerable stars and vast extent of the wide-open space around them. "My grandfather's grandfather was also chief of our people. This was long ago, in a time when the doe and bear were not affected by white settlers."

Hakan continued with a sad face, one that was clearly in love with that lost world. "One day, a new Indian visit our people from a tribe far to the east. This man talked with a snake's tongue, and he became trusted in our tribe."

Hakan spread out his hands, pointed to the east, as if expecting that long-ago figure to reemerge. He hesitated for a moment, lost in his thoughts.

"Go on, Chief," prompted Crook.

"Until my people became sick. Many died, and many went missing. It was a time of great suffering for the Hewisidawi," Hakan said, mulling over the torment his forefathers had experienced.

Hakan stared into the night, his demeanor sad, and it only grew worse with the telling of the story. "Nobody understood what was wrong, and many feared the end of tribe."

Hakan stopped, brooding as he mastered the sorrow of the moment. Focusing on his daughter, he nodded, as if what he explained next could only be understood by her, a member of his tribe.

"But my ancestors knew. The chief knew that evil had come into my people from outside," Hakan said. "He knew that that evil was from the Native visitor, from far away. And he knew he must destroy this snake-tongued outsider before everything was lost."

Frowning, Crook stood and paced around the limited space, focusing on Hakan as he pondered. "Your leader knew this evil Native was the cause of your tribe's troubles? What was done?"

"The chief spoke to the medicine man. They decided a plan to destroy the evil outsider, to kill him and throw him in the river with all his possessions. They did this, and after that, man from other tribe was never seen again by my people."

Crook found himself staring at Nayeli and had to drag his gaze away. Nayeli met his gaze without reservation, unafraid and seemingly...interested.

"Our people thrived until the white man came, many moons later," continued Hakan. "But my father told me that the outsider swore vengeance on the chief before he died. This foul Native said he would return to destroy us, no matter how much time had passed. He cursed us and this area."

Crook thought for a while, stepping carefully while considering the story. Coming to a stop, he leaned close to Hakan and spoke slowly, making sure the chief understood each word of his question. "Chief, is it now your opinion that this 'Chindi' has returned here? Merely to take his vengeance on your people?"

Nayeli answered the question, interrupting Crook's gaze with a rise in her voice. "Chindi is back. He has taken people from our other villages, making them into his demons. This is why some of our people attacked you and the settlers, thinking you were destroying us."

Hakan nodded in agreement. "This is why braves attacked settlers. This is what Chindi wants, to make hate between us. And then recently I saw the white men that take my people. They are possessed from that evil Native and they infect this land with new demons. They will also take your soldiers and turn this into an evil and suffering place. Nobody will survive Chindi's revenge."

Hakan stood, facing Crook directly. His face was full of conviction, showing no fear. He was not a man that lacked for fortitude. "So, we must go to your captain, otherwise all will be lost. Your 'Judah' must listen to us, and we must fight Chindi together. It is only way."

Turning away, Hakan walked abruptly to a pair of trees, where he lowered himself between them. Leaning into the darkness, he lay on his back and peered into the night sky.

Left behind, Nayeli remained seated and watched Crook suspiciously. Staring for some time, Crook remembered his manners and gestured toward her father. "Please, go and sleep, Nayeli. It has been a long day for us all. I will take first watch and we will wake you both in the morning."

Nayeli peered up at Crook, her beautiful face focusing on his. Confused, she considered whether he was friend or foe, glancing back and forth between Crook and the reclined image of Hakan in the nearby trees.

Nodding uncertainly, she walked away to join her father.

#

The day was without clouds or wind, an unusual occurrence for the local climate. The party of soldiers and Natives straddled the wide and dusty trail, looking apprehensively ahead. In shock, they traded worried glances with Crook.

Ahead of them was a stagecoach, lying broken and canted on its side across the trail. Its harnesses had attachments for horses, but none were currently there—either alive or dead.

Loraine fixed an intimidating stare on Hakan, unspoken blame boiling from his rigid face. He spat a glob of tobacco to punctuate his contempt for the chief.

Hakan shook his head, neither afraid nor worried about the sergeant. "This is not from my people. All of tribe has left this area."

Crook gestured to the wrecked conveyance, his voice monotoned and depressed. "That is the stage that brings mail and news from all the forts to the east, when not of a military nature. It brings civilian visitors too. So, there should be at least some passengers on board, along with the driver and guard."

Loraine walked into the field on the side, holding up his musket and scanning the rolling meadows. Not seeing any threats, he nodded toward Crook.

"Privates Blenchley and Trumain, please investigate the coach for survivors. Ensure you are careful in doing so," Crook ordered.

Trumain and Blenchley crept up the trail, approaching the broken vehicle with muskets raised. As they arrived at the lonely coach, Trumain tilted his weapon to point into the dark confines of its broken interior.

Trumain stared into the darkness with scared eyes, expecting the worst. After a moment, he lowered the musket and shook his head back at the party.

The rest of the group joined the privates, carefully moving up and examining the shattered coach. Blood was splashed across much of the exterior, and women's clothing and personal goods were strewn throughout the inside.

There was also a child's doll on the broken seat in the back compartment, looking like it has been dipped in black gore. Grabbing the doll, Loraine handed it to Crook.

The rest of the soldiers examined the supplies from the top of the coach, checking through packed bags and blankets, while Hakan and Nayeli stared worriedly across the desolate surrounding fields.

Horrified, Crook turned the toy over in his hands. He spoke low so that only Loraine could hear him. "Corporal Hollis's parents were supposed to visit before the winter, correct? Did he also refer to a young cousin that might accompany them?"

Loraine took a deep breath, acknowledging Crook with a nod but not responding openly. Several moments passed between the two as they considered the tragic possibilities.

Crook frowned and panned his eyes to the rest of the group, making sure they all were out of earshot. "Let us keep this between us, Sergeant; there's no need to tell anyone until we know the facts...of this matter."

Taking the doll from Crook, Loraine tucked it into a pouch. His gaze fell on Trumain as the private approached the sergeant and Crook.

Frustrated and worried, Trumain held up a small suitcase. "Sergeant, just a bunch of bags, civilian ones. Also, food and water."

Loraine spoke louder now, addressing the entire group. "Leave all the bags, and only bring supplies of food and water if you need them."

Trumain nodded but looked like he wanted to say more.

Loraine motioned for him to talk. "What is it?"

"I'm just wondering how we can fight these...things. How can we win against something like this?"

Clenching his jaw, Loraine approached the despairing soldier, getting up close. As Trumain tried to avoid Loraine's stare, Loraine moved his face to follow Trumain's gaze.

"We fight like soldiers. We kill them just like we did at the creek, by destroying or severing their heads. Most important, we never give an inch. Never give up, or you're already dead. Weakness breeds death. Am I understood?"

Crook cleared he throat, speaking softer than Loraine. "It really is that simple, Private. We shall hope for the chance to strike them down—without the fiends killing us in turn."

After a moment of shame, Trumain nodded. Raising his eyes to Loraine, he assumed a more confident demeanor and returned to the coach to gather more supplies.

Beckoning for the chief and Nayeli to join them, Crook looked down the endless trail of rolling fields and windswept prairies. If not for the shocking circumstances of their travel, the remote area would have retained a pleasant and raw beauty, offering a chance to enjoy the wide-open and raw nature of an environment that was unchanged for thousands of years.

As the tired troopers and their reluctant Indian allies gathered around, Crook motioned the party forward with a determined grimace.

#

The group trudged ahead, making their way across a vast mountain meadow filled with dirty scrub. Loraine was in front, keeping his attention to the swaying grass on either side as he searched for any potential ambush. Behind him was Crook, followed by the other soldiers.

Brush and foliage swayed in the wind as they passed.

Hakan and Nayeli were in the back, and they strode with the practiced ease of people who made their lives on the trail. No fatigue crossed their faces, and the blowing dust from the rangy trail didn't appear to affect their vision. They walked like statues, peaceful and unmoved by the isolated surroundings.

Ahead loomed Fort Hollenbush, set in the middle of a wide and treeless stretch of meadow. From the outside, it was imposing in its own way, especially considering its remote location. The log walls were attractive and welcoming on the secluded field, providing a sense of civilization to the otherwise-isolated expanse of high-mountain scenery.

The travelers plodded toward its wooden gates, and an anonymous figure above the heavy-doored entrance noted their approach with gyrating arms. Distant shouts from sentries accompanied the movement.

Crook called a halt to group. He raised his voice to be heard over howling prairie gusts. "Our journey ends soon, and we can get some rest and food. Please, say nothing of our fight to the other men. I will report to Captain Judah, and we shall contemplate the best course of action, but I do not wish to create panic before that time."

Loraine scowled, and nobody else appeared fond of that course of action. Their faces showed Crook he had exactly zero chance of keeping the trip's tragic events secret.

Frowning, Crook sighed and walked to the gate, where he held his hand up in greeting to the sentry.

Staring down from the parapet on the wall was Childs. The always-sarcastic private raised his voice, smiling intently and grinning at Crook. "Lieutenant, glad to see you. Where is everyone? Pugh? Thompson?"

Crook was surprised by the second name, shooting Loraine a concerned glance as he absorbed the absence of the men he left with the horses. Loraine was equally distraught but avoided addressing the obvious as he also stared up at Childs.

"I had hoped Privates Thompson and Cooper would have returned by now," Crook remarked, offering a grim expression.

Breathing deep, Crook lowered and shook his head, as if trying to find something positive to say from their tragic expedition.

After a tortured pause, Crook addressed Childs with a solemn frown. "I am afraid we have had some casualties, Private, and in any case, we do not bring back good tidings."

Childs' smirk melted away, and he stared at the bedraggled group, taking in the names of those that were currently absent. Coming to his senses, he motioned behind the wall, and the gate swung open with a scraping clatter.

As the group entered the wide-open space beyond the entrance to the fort, several soldiers on the drilling field focused on them. Stopping their duties, each of the men moved their gaze around the group, puzzled by what they saw.

Due to the presence of the Natives and with four troopers missing, none of the observers appeared happy. In fact, their sour expressions could only mean they were exceptionally angry—and didn't hide it.

It was not a welcoming or warm greeting.

Crook felt their stares, and his normally composed expression was overwhelmed by a blush. Not one to dwell on emotion, he tried ignoring the spectacle and strode ahead.

Hakan wasn't surprised and didn't flinch from the attention surrounding him and Nayeli. Leaning toward his daughter, he removed a beaded necklace from over his head and dropped it around Nayeli's neck.

Nayeli seemed surprised by the strange gesture but smiled at her father. Being in the camp of her tribe's former enemies did not leave a good impression, particularly as the eyes of the young soldiers sought to blame someone for their recent losses, but she also knew her father needed help to defeat their otherworldly enemy.

Sensing her anxiety, Hakan put a reassuring hand on Nayeli's shoulder and squeezed. Keeping a concerned smile, she nodded appreciation for the gesture and leaned close to him, as if his close proximity could mitigate the difficult situation around them.

Private Jackson stepped out from the guardhouse and walked toward the party. The rigid trooper carried a clinking chain of iron handcuffs, and he paced toward Hakan with deliberateness.

Crook waved him off, shaking his head in the process.

Jackson looked around in confusion.

"That will not be necessary, Private. The chief is unarmed and has been a great help to us. I will take responsibility."

"S-Sir?" asked Jackson. "We have orders to—"

"I know what your orders are, Private," replied Crook, a hint of warning in his voice. "But you have not seen what we have, and in any case, he will be staying with me in my quarters."

Crook motioned to Nayeli. "With his daughter."

Appearing even more perplexed, Jackson spun around for a moment, as if an explanation for Crook's orders would suddenly fall from the sky. Sighing, he retreated to the guardhouse as he shook his head.

Loraine was surprised by the encounter and met Crook's eyes with a questioning look.

Shaking his head at the sergeant, Crook raised his voice and spoke in a clear and officious manner. "Gentlemen, please store your equipment and get to your quarters for some well-deserved rest. You have been through a horrible trial, but I fear there will be more to come. Tomorrow, I will come to you to discuss our...expedition."

Relieved, the four remaining soldiers of the mission dispersed quickly. Confused, Loraine cast a puzzled glance backward as he stalked toward the barracks.

Getting the attention of Hakan and Nayeli, Crook pointed across the dusty communal area to his quarters. Walking determinedly, he ignored the continuing stares of the camp's soldiers as the Natives followed him across the interior of the compound.

Chapter 6

The moonlight brightened the remote stretch of trail, with patches of dim light illuminating clumps of brush and grass across the well-worn path. Fog covered the landscape in stretches, and the fields surrounding the overturned stagecoach were empty.

Silence and gloom filled the dead of night.

Far down the trail, a distant movement crossed the murky pathway. Barely visible outlines milled about in the fog, as if they were hazy spirits without material substance.

Multiple fiends materialized from the blackness, slogging quietly with almost mechanical gaits from the low-hanging mist shrouding the ground. As the gaggle of devilish creatures emerged from the darkness, they walked with determination and focus.

They were led by the hideous Chindi, who also walked with an unnatural and plodding shuffle. The wretched demon moved deliberately, not unlike a man, but also something much more—and far worse.

The group following their malevolent leader grew in number, stretching in a line along the long trail. Their feet slapped across the wet ground, and their soulless eyes panned from side to side as they searched for new prey.

As Chindi got close to the coach, he stopped to take in its destruction. Reaching inside the abandoned compartment, he pulled out a woman's bonnet from a tattered and bloodied supply of personal garments.

The head covering was drenched in blood, and Chindi's gray fingers massaged the material as he turned it over in his deathly hands. His white eyes searched the area, looking for something as they scoured the surrounding darkness. Turning in a circle, he faced south in the directionless night.

Expectantly, Chindi waited.

After several minutes, vague figures emerged on the periphery of the night's darkness. The outlines of Corporal Hollis's parents became visible, with his mom dressed in an expensive dress, while the father trudged forward in a dapper suit. Neither of their ghastly faces appeared proud of their formerly pleasant clothing, as the material was now splattered with their own dark gore. Each showed grave wounds across their torsos, yet they did not appear bothered by the mortal injuries.

As they advanced, they focused on Chindi, as if wishing to embrace their foul overlord. Stopping short of him, they were quiet, swaying in the shadowed night.

Chindi idly watched them, then transferred his gaze to the shattered stagecoach. Something like a smile crossed his putrid black lips as he considered his hellish new minions.

Facing ahead, Chindi stood still for a time. The backdrop of his followers was silent as they awaited his otherworldly intentions.

With a nod, Chindi moved ahead, leading the vile group down the same trail Crook recently used, toward the fort that housed the few survivors of the recent fight with his possessed monsters.

As they trudged ahead, the devilish cadre of creatures followed without question. Nobody argued or whined. Nobody joked.

Nobody said anything, and the former Natives and white men slogged into the darkness, united in their common and unholy cause.

#

The night was crisp, and a chill autumn wind blew over the walls of the isolated fort. Signal fires burned at periodic points along the interior of the wooden wall, and several sentries hovered near the flames, hunched against the cold and rubbing their hands to keep warm.

Crook stepped into the night from his quarters, appearing unbothered by the frigid weather. Behind him, light escaped from the windows of the small officers' quarters, and the outline of Nayeli's thin frame watched him through the frosty windowpane.

Crook angled toward the front gate, where two soldiers stood near one of the fires.

Crook was purposely friendly as he approached, affecting a kind demeanor and raising his voice to a cordial tone. "Corporal Hollis, it is good to see you. It is perhaps not the best of times for our soldierly efforts, but we are fortunate to have men such as you to guard the frontiers."

Looking surprised, Hollis glanced around, thinking for a moment Crook may have been talking to someone else.

Hollis stumbled over his words, and the cold temperature made it hard for him to speak properly. "Thanks, Lieutenant, I'm...err, just doin' my job. Hate when the weather turns cold like this."

Crook moved near the flames, nodding genially. Holding his hands up to catch the fire's heat, he politely motioned for the other soldier, a bored private with the last name of Hawthorne, to move along. As the man walked away, Crook stepped close to Hollis and lowered his voice.

"It is essential for us to keep on guard as we monitor the situation in this area. The last several days have taught us that peril lurks in each area we patrol."

Hollis tilted his head to the side, as if he wasn't getting Crook's point. "I thought it was the Indians who were attacking us. Why are they now acting like devils? Some of the other lads are sayin' they're like monsters, looking to make us into their slaves. Who ever heard anything like that?"

Crook frowned, showing his displeasure at the already-disseminated rumors. "We're not yet sure—"

"Word is, we're under attack from some Indian demon," Childs interrupted, pacing from the darkness and nodding mischievously to Crook. "And nobody knows where it came from—or how to fight it."

Childs accentuated his rumor-mongering with a shit-eating grin, tilting his head to appear friendly.

Crook offered Childs a stern glare but otherwise stayed quiet, while Hollis' bulging eyes showed his inclination to pummel him at a later time. Care-free and happy, Childs continued his grin and didn't flinch from their reprimanding looks.

"Childs, were you born with your big mouth, or did it develop over time?" asked Hollis, and he inched closer to the private, getting ready to box his ears.

Crook sighed, exhaling in a long, controlled breath. "Private Childs is entitled to his knowledge, however limited it may be. But the reality is we don't yet precisely know what enemy we face, except that they are some variety of hellish spawn. Fortunately, whatever it is, it can and already has been killed. What we have already slain, we can certainly kill again."

Childs met Crook's gaze, unsatisfied for the moment with the explanation. "Word also is Lieutenant Crook had to hack the head off an Indian to stop it, even while it was killin' Evans. Took him a bunch of slices to take the Native's head. How we gonna fight against something like that?"

Crook said nothing as he stared into the flames, pondering Childs' words. He focused on the embers for several moments, mulling the direction of the conversation and how easy gossip tended to travel in a small outpost like this. Not that he could blame them, but he still felt it necessary to control the mood of the fort; otherwise, discipline could become harder to maintain.

Coming to a decision, he nodded at Childs, then Hollis. "Your information is true, Private, but your efforts would be best focused on readying for battle, instead of instilling panic. We managed to return here, in spite of the odious enemy we faced. Survival favors the bold on this frontier, not those who would cower in fear."

Crook reached out, affectionately grasping Hollis on the shoulder. Sadly, he left his hand there, considering something more. "I would have you know, both of you, that we are in this together. We will take care of each other, no matter who or what we face. No matter...the losses."

With that, Crook smiled grimly at Hollis and nodded in empathy. Hollis missed Crook's indirect condolences as he shivered against the cold.

Childs dropped his challenging gaze to the fire and went quiet. Chewing on his lip, he wondered what else he could say to piss Hollis off.

After a moment, Crook nodded politely and pivoted away from the fire.

As Crook paced into the night toward the headquarters building, Childs and Hollis swapped worried glances, like they were not quite sure why the lieutenant just visited.

#

Judah propped himself at his desk, peering down at some crinkled papers. Rubbing his eyes, he mumbled a series of unintelligible grunts as he read. His expression was confused as his eyes darted about the page of neat cursive writing.

Shuffling the papers to the side, Judah fumbled out his pocket watch. Staring weirdly, he moved his head back to focus his middle-aged eyes on the dials of the timepiece. It was 6:00 PM.

A tap came from the door, and Judah waited a moment before responding, taking a deep breath to prepare for what was coming. His face was a mixture of anger and apprehension as he stared expectantly ahead.

"Enter," Judah said, showing no enthusiasm for the invite.

Crook strode into the room, calm and in pristine military dress. His whiskers were in perfect order, and his uniform was flawless. Saluting, he stood at formal attention.

"At ease, Lieutenant," said Judah.

Judah stood and walked to the unflappable Crook. He crowded close to his subordinate, looking intently into Crook's detached gaze.

Glancing at Judah's watery and bloodshot eyes, Crook didn't appear in the least concerned with Judah's bullying posture.

Judah pointed to the window, raising his voice. "What in the hell are you thinking? I told you that I wanted that man hung."

Judah paced away, then swung his attention back to Crook. He throttled down his emotions, trying to control his temper, but the effect on his face just made him look more frenzied. "And now he's in your quarters instead, with his daughter attached."

Keeping his cool, Crook maintained a calm voice. "I have told you precisely what transpired, Captain Judah. Please, do tell me why you want to pursue your former intentions."

Crook met Judah's gaze. Now, it was Crook that challenged Judah, and his steely eyes begged Judah to contradict him concerning the recent events.

After a war of stares, Judah surrendered and returned to his seat, plopping down into the wooden chair.

"You have offered me stories of monsters and death," said Judah. "You've lost four men—"

"Two for certain, Captain," interrupted Crook. "But I fear for the others in this foul climate. They are long overdue."

"Four men. And what maniac would believe such abject nonsense?" asked Judah. "We are losing our men and have no aid forthcoming. Where will we get more help?"

Judah buried his face in his hands and rubbed his eyes. Taking a moment to collect himself, Judah returned his stare to Crook. Appearing resigned to his fate, he spoke in a flat manner. "We were due to receive reinforcement from Fort Bidwell, in the form of Lieutenant Gardiner and his platoon of Dragoons. But now they are long overdue."

Crook's gaze sharpened at this. He took a step forward, surprising Judah.

"If they came from Fort Bidwell, that means they would have had to traverse the area where we just encountered our...troubles," Crook said, thinking out loud. "Perhaps they encountered the same enemy?"

Crook walked to a map on the wall, where he ran his finger over various figures of troop dispositions and landmarks to their west.

"Captain Judah, this situation is now dire," Crook said, turning around and facing his commander. "I have been to the empty village of the chief, and I have seen the regular stagecoach destroyed on the trail leading here."

Crook approached the desk, placing his hands on it and leaning down to focus on Judah. "We must immediately abandon this post and flee east. We have to warn the army what is happening."

Suddenly finding his courage, Judah held up a silencing finger. "Are you insane? Abandon this fort? Am I the only officer in the history of the army to lose his command to...demons?"

Standing erect, Crook forced himself to remain calm, controlling the urge to throttle Judah. "Captain Judah, the people of this country need to be warned. It would appear that hell itself is opening, and they—"

"Hell?" Judah asked, his voice growing irate. "Do you hear yourself, Lieutenant? I would be shot for desertion."

"Captain, if we stay here, I fear we will not live to worry about discipline," Crook replied. "I have never run from a conflict in my military life—"

Judah slammed his fist on the desk and rose from his defeatist stupor. "And you will not run now, either. We will stay here. We will fortify the post and keep ourselves safe. In the spring, we will make contact with command—or await relief. We will survive..."

Judah didn't look like he believed his own words. His eyes darted up to his favorite painting, but the woman depicted therein didn't seem interested in his troubles.

Crook breathed deep, considering the situation. Choosing an internal decision he could comfortably deal with, his expression turned to indifference. "Fair enough, Captain Judah, we shall do as you say."

Keeping his tone artificially respectful, Crook motioned with his head to the door. "And I shall prepare the men for a siege."

Judah peered up at Crook, suddenly suspicious of his acquiescence. Standing from behind the desk, he stepped gently forward, lowering his voice to a friendly tone. "Lieutenant Crook, we will find a way through this...problem. As officers, we must stand strong..."

As Judah trailed off, Crook said nothing more. His face was a mask of submissiveness, but his disrespect for Judah was a secret to neither of them.

Sighing, Judah dismissed Crook, who saluted and left the room.

When he was gone, Judah's gaze moved to the map on the wall and the marked military units. His distressed eyes moved from one unit designation to another, and he mentally focused on them, as if doing so would somehow bring more help to his remote command.

#

Fatigued, Loraine sat at a crude table in the noncommissioned officers' barracks. It was a functional room filled with simple wood furnishings and personal effects.

Some colored paintings of indeterminate cities hung on one wall, while two others were adorned with rosters and numerous post orders. Four simple beds lay spaced out against the far wall, all of which were tidy and inspection-ready.

Holding a quill, Loraine sighed as he looked down. Scrawled in presentable handwriting on a clean sheet was a letter.

Dear Mrs. Selby,

It is with great sadness that I wish to inform you of the death of your son, Private Selby. He fell in action while fighting to protect peaceful settlers against the savages that plague this portion of our great nation. He is an honor to his family and will be missed by his comrades. I had not known your son long, but...

Frustrated, Loraine set the quill in its holder. Standing, he moved to the far end of the room, where he crossed his arms and stared at personnel rosters hanging on a nail.

Grasping the papers, he shuffled through them as he tried to figure something out. Flipping the sheets over, he still didn't find what he was looking for, and he set the jumbled sheaves aside.

From the front entrance came a hard knock, and Loraine stared in confusion at the door. "Yes? Come in."

Crook strode into the room, and the door clacking against the wall was testimony to his brusqueness.

Surprised, Loraine watched Crook in baffled silence. He raised an inquisitive eyebrow to the lieutenant, but the intended effect was lessened by his caterpillar-like unibrow.

"Sir? You've never come in here before," Loraine said. "You could've sent a runner…"

Crook held up a hand to silence Loraine, trying to be polite but mostly failing. Stepping near the sergeant, Crook dropped four envelopes onto the wooden table, where they landed next to Loraine's condolence letter. The envelopes were thick and sealed with wax.

"Sergeant Loraine, please pick four of your best riders and have each of them take one of these letters," said Crook. "Tonight— immediately."

Loraine's perplexed look continued as he stared at the letters.

"Lieutenant, why…what is the purpose…?" asked Loraine, looking up at Crook.

Crook walked close to Loraine, where he spoke in a barely controlled voice. "Two of the riders are to go east, directly toward Camp Sadler. Two are to go west, to Fort Bidwell, but they must take the long route to the south to get there. All four are to travel separately, to increase their chances of success. They must give these letters in person to the commanding officers, with no exception."

Crook walked back to the table, where his eyes fell on Loraine's letter. His demeanor softened as he skimmed the words.

Looking back up, Crook met Loraine's confused stare. He lightened his features, trying to appear kind. "Have one of those going to Camp Sadler take the Scott daughter with him. She cannot stay here under any circumstances."

Loraine moved back to the table, taking in Crook's words with each step. He nodded to Crook as he got close to him, laying down the rosters he was examining.

Loraine's eyes glazed over as he considered something, and he gestured to the half-written letter, changing the subject. "Lieutenant, for yet another time in my army career, I have to write a letter to a mother of another dead soldier, in this case, Selby. One thing I've found is that there are always more letters like this as the years wear on."

Loraine pointed to a dresser in the corner, where a stack of more empty sheets of paper awaited his death notifications.

"It is the nature of our profession, Sergeant," Crook responded. "It is certainly unfortunate but necessary if we are to do any good in this world."

Loraine shook his head, and his jaw appeared set against the words as he talked. He gestured to the rosters on the table. "That's not my point, Lieutenant. My problem is that I can no longer remember their first names. I have to write letters, and I can't find their names. That young boy is cold flesh in our burying place, and I can't think of his damn name. His mother gets a letter where he's only 'Private Selby.' Is this the honorable life that we're supposed to be leading? Aren't these young men known enough by us to even have a name?"

Crook's thinking slowed down as he took in Loraine's intent. At a loss to say anything, he became quiet. Staring at the roster, he didn't know how to respond, and he assumed the look of someone who just learned something new.

Being caught up in the military his entire adult life, Crook was a man who was driven to complete his mission with honor, to stand and fight for that which was honorable and just. In all that time, he had never stopped to think about something as simple as what a young man next to him was called by their family.

The presence of soldiers was meant to accomplish a mission, either by providing security to an insecure population or by enforcing the will of orders on wayward miscreants with the boot of raw force. It hadn't occurred to Crook that something more was called for because *this is what we do.*

Still, Crook, for all his faults, knew that the world around him was created for purposes beyond his understanding, which meant he could afford to learn some compassion as he worked through his duties.

In this case, it meant paying attention to the simple name of a young man who died doing his duty. Chagrined, Crook whispered a reply. "It was Nathaniel. Private Nathaniel Selby."

Loraine nodded, smiling with a distant look as he remembered the too-skinny soldier. His eyes teared up, but he was suddenly happier.

Coming back to the moment, his voice returned to normal, and he looked anew at Crook's letters. "What did Judah say?"

Quieter now, Crook was still exasperated, but he was also calmer. "He thinks we should die rather than inform the world of what is transpiring here. That is... unacceptable."

Loraine considered a moment and shook his head with disapproval at that outcome. Moving quickly, he retrieved his overcoat from a hook on the wall and collected Crook's letters on his way to the door.

"One more thing, Sergeant," said Crook.

As Loraine stopped and waited, Crook took out his revolver, checking the cylinder and bore for proper alignment.

Re-holstering the weapon, Crook stared at Loraine with clear eyes, eyes that held no self-doubt or worries about their direction. "Judah may not care if staying here means we forfeit our lives. But I do. Tomorrow at eighteen hundred hours come to my quarters with O'Rourke, Trumain, and Blenchley."

Crook gestured to the window, pointing outside to the darkness. His tone was uncompromising. "If we must stay, we will not die like lambs. We will go out and take the fight to these devils. Never in military history did a timid soldier carry the day in battle against a violent aggressor."

In response, Loraine watched Crook and pondered his words. As the moments passed, his face grew more approving of the lieutenant, and he nodded with enthusiasm at the sentiment to take the fight to their wicked enemy.

Smiling grimly, Loraine exited the room, leaving Crook alone in his empty quarters.

#

Chief Hakan peered down, a look of disbelief in his exasperated features. Raising his eyes to the wall, poignant anger filtered into his expression. He stewed in that anger before assuming the pose of an indignant and aggrieved victim.

"You didn't say horse could jump over castle," exclaimed Hakan. "What horse can jump over such large building?"

Across a small table from Hakan, Crook grinned down at the chessboard and took the chief's last protective pawn.

"Checkmate, Chief," Crook said, his smile growing wider. "You must now concede the board."

As Crook toppled Hakan's king, Nayeli snickered a few feet away with a playful look on her face. She glanced back and forth between Crook and Hakan, holding obvious affection for both. As they returned her stare, the feeling was clearly mutual.

"I told you, Father, never play the white man's game. They only tell you rules after they've won," Nayeli said.

Hakan feigned anger and smiled, but there was also a hint of real irritation concerning her words. "That is true, Crook. Every time our tribe agrees to new rules, the white man changes them—and nobody tell us."

Crook's happy expression faded away, but he spoke in a convicted and respectful tone. "I agree, Chief. There is a problem of mistrust on both sides because I do not control every white man, and you don't hold sway over every Indian. In my view, we must not force you to take our civilization immediately in its complete form, but under just laws, guaranteeing to Indians equal civil laws. The Indian question, a source of such dishonor to this country and a shame to true patriots, will hopefully be a thing of the past as we move forward."

Both Nayeli and Hakan spent time absorbing Crook's speech. Each was unsure of the truth behind Crook's words, but they also didn't doubt his noble intentions.

Looking uncomfortable, Hakan sighed and stood. "You think we want to be part of your world, Crook? My people live here long before your White Father or his city existed."

Crook's response was to drop his eyes in disappointment, bringing an odd calm to the room.

Reconsidering the delivery of his viewpoint, Hakan softened his expression and tried to moderate his words. "Yet, if peace came from you or white father, I would be more confident of your words, Crook. But I fear other men have more power to harm my people."

Hakan gestured toward the door, which faced Judah's quarters across the wide interior of the military post. Nayeli nodded her agreement with her father's reluctance to trust Judah, and her worried stare found Crook.

Crook kept his tone warm, trying to appear sure of an outcome that could keep them both happy—or at least not at a state of war. "Well, if we can only focus on what unites us—"

A hard rap on the door interrupted the conversation. Looking surprised, Crook glanced down to his pocket watch and noted the time. Nodding carefully, he moved to the door and swung it gently inward.

Peeking in from the night were Loraine, O'Rourke, Trumain, and Blenchley.

Crook quietly ushered them into the room, where they spread out and filled up most of the available space. Nayeli made some effort to stay close to Crook in the gaggle of people, and Crook responded by keeping her close by his side.

Clapping Loraine on the shoulder, Crook then motioned to an expansive map on the wall. The group crowded around it, studying the contours of the land and various place names, such as "Tall Indian Gulch" and "Screaming Child's Fork."

Hakan hung back from the press of people, appearing uncomfortable in the tight quarters. His eyes jumped around, as if searching for something, and he glanced nervously out the window.

Crook pointed at the map, offering his best professorial tone to the varied group. Speaking slowly, he indicated their current position. "Are there any suggestions for how we can best fight our common enemy?"

Hakan replied from the back of the party, his voice strained and sad. "You must avoid Chindi's devils. Don't get close to them, or they turn you to demon. It is better to die than become his slave."

Private O'Rourke spoke up, sounding well-rested but still worried. "Yeah, we saw what they can do, but if you can bash 'em in the head really hard or hit them with a good musket shot, that stops 'em cold. It ain't pretty, but it works."

Crook smiled, giving O'Rourke a supportive glance. "Which is why I asked you all to come here tonight. It is only those in this room that have survived a clash with our wicked foe. We shall have to put our experience in fighting them to good use in the future. Soon, perhaps."

None of the assembled party appeared excited by that prospect.

Crook pointed again to the map and traced his fingers across multiple contour lines of the yellowed paper. He gestured at a remote area called "Burney," then moved his attention back to where they now stood, "Fort Hollenbush."

"We can assume they have the entire area here to Burney Meadows under their control," said Crook. "And they have spread out from there, toward this fort. It is likely we are their next intended victims."

Appearing disturbed, Hakan made his way to the map, pushing through the gaggle of bodies. Loraine looked annoyed as he brushed by.

"You are brave to fight them, Crook, but you must kill Chindi himself to beat them," Hakan said. "When you kill other demons, they just return to dark place you call hell."

"The problem with that, Chief, is that this Chindi can make new devils as fast as Sam Colt makes his revolvers," retorted Loraine, and the other troopers grunted in agreement.

Nodding, Hakan raised his voice to be heard above the murmured chatter. "This is true. You must kill white man who has Chindi in him. Then you must bury his body in old Indian burial ground at Pit River. This is only way to stop Chindi."

Considering Hakan's words, Crook stared at each of the natives and soldiers in turn. Referring back to the map, he traced a route toward the Pit River.

Taking his cue, Hakan moved next to Crook and pointed at a specific portion of the river on the map. Keeping his finger on that point, he tapped it until Crook placed a pin there.

Stepping back, Crook concentrated and did mental calculations for the distance to the remote location. Nobody else appeared to have anything to add, and the room stayed quiet as the party members contemplated the task ahead.

Sighing, Crook paced the remaining area of quarters, focusing down at each step while considering their predicament. His boots scraped against the floor as his companions watched expectantly.

Hesitating for a moment, Crook looked uncertain as he scanned the rest of the group's faces. When his gaze stopped on Nayeli, he stared into her almond eyes, lost for a moment. His attraction to the Native woman did not go unnoticed, and Loraine rolled his eyes at the budding romance.

Embarrassed, Crook refocused on the mission at hand before speaking out. "This entire enterprise sounds like a good idea. The question is: how do we get the demon to follow us eighty-five miles to that burial ground?"

#

Private Steadman peered down from the top of the log wall that surrounded the main gate of Fort Hollenbush. Looking to the inside of the barrier, his features twisted into a confused frown.

Darkness surrounded his post at the main entrance to the fort, but Steadman was more interested in looking inside than watching the open fields around the structure. Outside the fort, moonlight made the grasslands easy to see—far into the distance.

"Ain't no way that really happened," said Steadman. "He's full of shit. He wouldn't know the truth if it bit him on the ass."

Below him, Private Childs held his hands over the spotting fire near the main gate. The flames blazed from their enclosure, lighting up the immediate area with some intensity.

Childs chuckled, barely able to hold the large musket he cradled in his well-clothed arms. In one hand he held a half-eaten cracker. "I swear it on my momma's grave, even if she ain't dead. In fact, if it ain't true, I'll go so far as to tell Sergeant Loraine what a mean bastard he is."

Steadman cackled down from his elevated position, shaking his head energetically. "Nah, you don't got no death wish. Sergeant will beat yer ass for sure. Remember what he did to Torrell when he talked back to him?"

"That's my point, ya brain-dead prairie rat," said Childs. "I wouldn't say it if I was lying."

The slower-than-normal Steadman thought on this for a moment, looking puzzled. Coming to a conclusion, he nodded. "Yeah, maybe you're right, then."

"Right about what?" asked Hollis, striding up from the well-lit gatehouse near the fire. "What are you two jabbering on about?"

Hollis moved next to Childs, blowing through his hands and crowding in for warmth.

"Corporal Hollis, Childs keeps talking about what Fritz saw at the river last week," says Steadman. "At least what he said he saw."

Hollis stared back and forth between the privates. Clearly unsure of what they were discussing, he gave Childs an intense stare, urging him to speak up with his bulging eyes.

Childs sighed, shaking his head and throwing what was left of his snack into the fire. Preparing for his story, his voice was mysterious and overly dramatic.

"All right, Corporal, it went down like this, I swear on—" began Childs.

"Get on with it, ya pea brain," replied Hollis. "We ain't got all night."

Feigning hurt, Childs motioned to the fort's interior. "OK, Fritz was making the run over to the Potter farm, the one near that ruined building near the river. Potter works on some of our stuff. Shines things up, repairs chains, that kinda thing. He's been there—"

"I know who Potter is; get on with it," demanded Hollis.

Childs paused before resuming his steady tone. "Anyway, so Fritz gets over there and he's gotta take a crap, so he goes down by the river, where there's a bunch of reeds and stuff to hide himself."

"Why did I know one of your stories would involve bowels, Childs?" Hollis asked, shaking his head.

Undeterred, Childs continued. "And so, he's squatting there, straining cuz he can't..."

"That's all that hard tack," Steadman interrupted, grinning down at them. "That'll bind ya up for a week if ya eat too much. It's like eatin' baked sawdust."

Childs nodded and smiled up at Steadman. When he was about to say something, Hollis' scowl persuaded him to continue his story.

"So, Fritz is there doing his thing, and he notices someone splashin' in the water," said Childs. "He can't make out who it is, so he moves the weeds aside and peeks out, all while he's still squatting."

Steadman cackled again, making the sort of chuckle that could have driven someone to murder. He went quiet when Hollis glared up at him.

Working up his tone for dramatic effect, Childs leaned into the fire, and his face was bathed in the flickering firelight. "And there she is, a beautiful naked squaw, skinny-dipping in the river. She was splashing water all over her...body."

Looking down, Steadman gulped, trying to come to terms with the magnitude of a naked Native bathing in an area they'd lived in for thousands of years.

"Tell him what happened next," Steadman said, staring with open eyes.

Hollis held his hand up to stop Childs, and his dubious glare grew more doubtful with each passing moment. "You desperate young soldiers just make it up as you go along. There aren't no naked squaws over by Potter's farm. That's nowhere near their villages."

"I ain't joshin' ya, Hollis, swear on my honor," Childs exclaimed. "It really happened."

"Tell the rest of it," Steadman said, focusing down at the pair and licking his lips eagerly.

Steadman seemed to have forgotten the purpose of guard duty and hadn't looked outside the walls for several minutes.

Hollis glared at each of them like a disapproving schoolmaster. Frustrated, he motioned for Childs to continue the story.

"All right. So, he's watching her, and all of the sudden she notices him in the bushes. She starts creeping up, trying to see who's watching her. Then, she sees it's one of us and starts screaming," said Childs, and he giggled as he continued. "She grabs a rock and runs at him while he's squatting. Chases him for about a mile, while she's naked and he's tryin' to pull up his pants. He never did make it to Potter's farm."

Steadman started laughing, and even Hollis couldn't stifle a grin as Childs joined in the chorus of chuckles.

After several moments of raucous snickers, their amusement died down. Both privates looked exhausted as their breathing returned to normal.

It was Hollis' turn to tell a story, and he leaned near the flames with a sparkling grin. "You know what? While you two only got stories, they got actual brothels down in San Francisco. Instead of terrorizing the Native women, you could actually go down there and...you know."

Childs' face became intrigued, as if he was pondering the secrets of life. His voice quivered. "B-brothels? They got those there? With real women?"

Hollis rolled his eyes, wondering if it was possible for a young man to be any more pathetic. His voice changed to a flat tone. "Yeah, they do. Problem is, you ain't never gonna get leave to go down there, cuz even the whores don't want no momma's boy, lovesick goat-herder in their houses of ill repute. You'd be bad for business. The real customers would be too busy laughing at you."

The night became silent, and both privates were crestfallen. Wrapped in their thoughts, they considered the possibilities of Hollis's words.

"Hollis, why couldn't I get stationed in San Francisco?" asked Childs. "Why do I gotta sit in the freezing mountains the rest of my life? I been here a year now. It ain't fair."

"Yeah, it ain't right," said Steadman from above, his features pursed into a sour expression. "And why do we always get guard duty? Ain't anyone else ever gonna get this cold gate under their feet?"

Hollis stared at each of the young soldiers, a wide smile crossing his whiskered face. "Because I gotta watch over you dumbshits for a living. It might as well be you. It just might do you some good—"

Abruptly, three loud raps came from the outside of the gate— firm and expectant knocks, from someone with a keen interest to enter the fort.

A soldier's hand was placed against the wood planks on the outside of the gate, pressing against the barrier. The rest of the man was unseen, apparently waiting for a reply.

Looking surprised, Steadman leaned out from the wall. After a quick glance down, he motioned back to Hollis and Childs.

"It's Thompson. He's made it back," exclaimed Steadman. "Hurry up and let him in. He's gotta be freezing."

Childs set his musket against the fort's interior wall. As he moved to withdraw the blocking arm from the gate, Hollis was uneasy. He glanced at Childs, raising his uncertain voice. "Childs, wait a minute. Why didn't Thompson call out?"

Above, Steadman twisted his face in a confused expression and glanced again outside. "What are you talking about, Hollis? It's Thompson. Thank God he's OK."

Childs kept dragging the wood, and the worried Hollis stepped forward, extending his arm to stop him. Hollis' fingers just touched Childs' shoulder.

The wooden block cleared the last metal joint and clattered to the side. Ignoring Hollis, Childs pulled on the gate with a grunt. The heavy barrier groaned as it slid open, and moonlight flooded through the opening.

Thompson stood there, backlit against the open and luminescent field behind him. His face wasn't yet visible in the dim light, and his shadowed features didn't move in greeting.

"Get in here and join us," said Childs. "You must be frozen stiff. The Lieutenant is gonna be—"

Thompson rushed forward, swinging a hand-ax down in a whirling arc. Thompson was now a Chindi-spawned wretch, and his dark complexion and heinous face flashed in the firelight, focusing entirely on the unsuspecting Childs.

The ax split Childs neatly between the eyes, burying to the hilt with the sound of ruptured wet fruit. Childs backpedaled, stumbling with the weapon stuck in his skull.

Childs tried to grab the ax, tried to say something, but only monotone gurgles escaped his astonished lips. Blood poured in sheets from the mortal wound, and he couldn't see anything around.

With his body not responding to his commands, Childs turned and shambled into the open ground of the fort. He struggled with each halting step, and a pathetic moan escaped his quivering lips.

Hollis watched the whole encounter, his eyes open in incomprehension. Staring at Childs stumbling away, he came to his senses and faced the possessed monster that was Thompson. Grabbing at the revolver in his holster, he struggled to smoothly extract it.

Hollis' eyes flashed in a fierce, roiling anger. Pulling out his weapon, he didn't shoot at Thompson, but instead rushed him with a bellowing cry.

Swinging the pistol butt-first, Hollis clobbered Thompson across the head, pushing him back out of the gate. He swung the weapon like a crazed madman, pummeling the creature across the face and neck with a series of jarring blows.

Above, Steadman broke free from his stupor and reached down for his musket. Pulling it to his shoulder, he saw a flood of figures running at the gate from across the field. He aimed down the large weapon, trying to pick out the best target.

The sounds of several arrows flitted through the air, and Steadman stared down at his shirt front, appalled and in shock.

Letting his weapon dangle in his off hand, Steadman couldn't come to terms with the shafts protruding from his chest. Reaching down, he tried to pull them out, but they were in too deep, stuck between his ribs and into his meaty internal organs. He agonized from the pain, swaying and trying to keep his balance from the sentry perch. His musket tumbled from his grip and clattered to the ground below.

Steadman stared up into the night, his eyes wide. Looking at the stars, they were beautiful and somehow eternal to the young trooper. A gentle smile crossed his lips, and he relaxed into a worry-free, dreamy state.

That smile was still on his dead face when he thudded on his back after tumbling off the wall.

At the gate barrier, Hollis managed to beat down the otherworldly Thompson, and he backed up as Thompson awkwardly tried to rise again.

Sprinting toward him from several directions across the open meadow were more creatures, all intent on his destruction. Glancing over, Hollis grabbed at the end of the gate, realizing it was the only hope for survival: *I gotta shut the gate.*

As he grasped its edge and began hauling the gate shut, he noticed the first of Chindi's minions coming at him from the darkness. It was not an Indian, or even a soldier...

It was his mom. She was dressed in a dirty dress, but nevertheless stood there in the flesh, watching him from her shadowed face.

Moved into inaction by the bizarre sight, Hollis let go of the gate. Struggling with himself, he took a halting step toward the possessed woman.

"Momma?" asked Hollis.

#

A musket blast echoed outside. Crook and the rest of the party looked away from the map, wide-eyed with alarm.

"They're already here," shouted Crook. "I had hoped for more of a delay."

Motioning to their weapons leaning against the wall, Crook pointed to the door. "Get your weapons and assemble outside. Be prepared for anything."

Hustling to grab their equipment, the companions scrambled around as they checked their weapons and ammunition in hurried order. Most showed fear in their eyes, though Hakan showed something more as he looked out the window.

The soldiers clambered out the door, with Loraine in the lead and shouting orders. "Move your asses, this is for it all. We'll send 'em back to hell."

Noise resounded from the rest of the camp as every building in the post awakened to the danger. Clamors of surging and confused voices emerged from the darkness all around.

As Hakan and Nayeli filed outside, Crook motioned for them to wait. Confused, the Natives stopped and watched him.

Crook moved to the wardrobe and flung the doors open. Reaching inside, he pulled out a pair of revolvers, offering one each to Nayeli and Hakan. They hesitated while looking down at the offered weapons.

"Take them," ordered Crook. "Hurry."

Reluctantly, each grabbed a pistol and hustled into the darkness. Crook followed them out, pushing his way to the front of his soldiers as they assembled in the dim night.

Glancing around, Crook saw the unfolding disaster for what it was. The gate stood ajar, and Hollis was there, wrestling with...his mother?

As if to accentuate the danger, a host of figures sprinted through the opening, bowling over Hollis, and the corporal was lost under the pile of horrific attackers.

Two soldiers rushed at the invaders with muskets raised, but they were hopelessly overmatched. Several more shots boomed through the rest of camp, with shrieks and screams coming from several directions.

"They've breached the gate," shouted Crook, and he pointed to the headquarters building. "Sergeant Loraine, assemble at the headquarters, we shall collect survivors and rally from there."

The party rushed across the field with overwhelmed looks, making their way for the headquarters. Looking determined, Loraine arrived first, where he pivoted and began arranging the men for battle.

The scared and panicked faces of the men were evident in the firelight, but Loraine was fearless as he shouted into their faces. "Never give up. Fight to the end, then fight some more. If an enemy can be seen, he can be killed. To live, you've gotta fight like the demons you see before you."

Crook rushed behind the men to Judah's door and beat wildly on it. His severe voice was loud and commanding as he pounded on the thick wood. "Captain Judah, it is time to face the enemy. Come out."

#

Judah could hear Crook beating on the door, but he simply didn't care at the moment. His ever-present whiskey glass was full, and his eyes were occupied as he focused on something far beyond the room he now sat in.

As Crook continued his assault on the door, Judah moved his stare again to the perfect painting hanging from his wall. His eyes examined every inch of the woman depicted, taking in her beauty and grace.

Her green eyes and fair skin were far more engaging and lifelike than anything possible with the recently invented technology of photography. With distant eyes, his mind took him back to another time.

#

Judah stopped at the perimeter fence, looking at the squat building set amidst pine trees and surging vegetation. It was daytime, and his home looked oddly alone, with the door ajar and no sounds emerging from inside. Nothing was visible in the dim area beyond the entrance, making the scene quiet and unsettling.

Standing behind him was Sergeant Holder, who crowded behind Lieutenant Judah. The brusque and burly Sergeant breathed deep, indicating intense exercise, as well as nervousness. He waited for Judah to give the order, clasping a heavy musket in his hands.

Judah gestured to his home and the duo sprinted for the door, making little effort to be quiet. As they got close, Judah stepped to the lead. Holding up his revolver, he pushed open the door, his face filling with acute dread.

The light from the doorway illuminated the back of the quaint house, falling across his beloved Sarah. Lying on her back in bed, her face was upside down and hung over the edge of the mattress. Mutilated and half-naked, her dead eyes were open and fixed on him.

Her strange unseeing gaze bored into Judah, as if blaming him for her distressed condition. Around her, sacks of food staples and personal items were cast about the room.

Her expression seemed to talk to Judah, as if to say "Welcome home, my love. Are you happy to see me this way? Maybe if you were here with me, I would be a little better off. What do you think, my love?"

Pushing past Judah, Sergeant Holder rushed to block Judah's view of his dead wife.

"It's those damnable outlaws from the gold fields," said Holder. "They've been preying on every settler this side of the valley."

Judah plopped down on his ass, dropping his weapon in his lap. His mind released its hold on sanity, and he stared up at Sergeant Holder with quivering eyes and blurred vision. The stare was of someone who no longer cared—and never would again.

#

Returning to his senses, Judah looked bleakly at the door. Tears ran down his face, freely flowing and unwiped. Crook still banged on the door, and Judah continued to ignore him.

Reaching out a shaking hand, Judah took a long sip of whiskey, grimly swallowing past a lump in his throat—a lump that had never gone away.

#

Crook strode away from the front of Judah's office, his expression wild and frustrated. Stepping in front of his men, he glanced again to the main entrance.

The attacking devils had overwhelmed the few defenders and were spreading throughout the fort. There were simply far too many to stop.

The new sounds of demonic wails resounded from bunches of men being held down on the field, announcing their induction into Chindi's hellish legion. Other devils sprinted off toward other buildings, their vague shapes looking predatory as the scampered ahead under the moonlight.

Crook stared in desperation at the evolving fight. His men were being butchered, with the few remaining troopers fleeing from the clutches of the unholy creatures.

Crook's expression became unsure, and he glanced about, searching for a way to prevail—to fight this unnatural invasion.

Loraine moved close, yelling in Crook's face and grabbing his shoulder. "What do we do, Lieutenant?"

From the other side, Nayeli grabbed his arm. Her face was less demanding but no less serious as she pled with him. "If we die here, Crook, all die. You will not stop Chindi here. We must go from this place."

Crook looked back to the main field. Childs was there, still stumbling in the darkness, dead on his feet but not yet knowing it. The young private haltingly grabbed at the ax in his head, and his groans of agony were almost as unnerving as the unnatural sounds from the demons around him.

Crook collected himself, biting back his sorrow as he came to a decision. "Sergeant, a retreat to the back entrance. We'll exit from there into the night."

Loraine nodded and grabbed Trumain by the collar, shouting and shoving him into O'Rourke and Blenchley. "Get moving to the back entrance. We're getting the hell outta here."

As the companions spun about and stumbled into the night, Hakan grabbed Crook's arm. With a strange expression, he glared into Crook's distraught eyes. "They will follow me, Crook. Chindi will follow me."

Crook was perplexed, but he nodded at Hakan, motioning for him and Nayeli to follow the soldiers. In a line, the group ran into the darkness, angling toward the back of the fort.

As they rushed through the night, more sounds of demonic screams arose from behind them, and pained shrieks of agony and begging erupting from clusters of various survivors.

Scattered muskets boomed in the darkness, but not in enough numbers to make a difference.

In a short time, the group made it to a massive iron door in the back wall of the fort. It was unguarded and sealed with a lock and heavy chain.

Crook gestured to Loraine, who nodded and raised his musket. The sergeant crashed the butt of his weapon against the rusted lock, and each of the party glanced back to the invaders, praying for it to break loose.

Each clanging strike brought more attention to the nervous group, and their window of opportunity for escape was closing with each passing moment.

After several more blows, the chain and lock finally broke away, and each companion was visibly relieved. Behind them, the screams died down. It had taken only minutes to conquer the fort.

Loraine hauled the creaking door open, revealing the pale night and calm fields beyond.

One-by-one, the companions scrambled into the darkness, keeping their eyes pointed ahead and rushing into the night. Behind them, Crook pulled the portal shut with clanking finality.

Crook, the last man to leave Fort Hollenbush alive, grimaced with anguish as he staggered after the remaining survivors.

#

At his desk, Judah stared at the last dose of whiskey in his glass. His depressed and sour features focused on the dark liquid, and he raised and swished around the remaining spirits.

Judah cradled the drink, his one source of refuge in the world, clasping it close to his chest as he contemplated his next move.

Around him, the room was unorganized and dirty. Documents and reports were stacked amongst personal goods and supplies with no sort of obvious order.

Outside, the screams of dying and possessed men were decreasing, and Judah realized his time was coming.

Judah finally wiped the drying tears from his face, and he stood from his desk with considerable effort.

Setting down the unfinished liquor, he straightened himself and looked about the room, as if he was suddenly unsure whether his quarters were inspection-ready. He smiled bitterly at the idea of an inspection, as he understood his years of sorrow and drunkenness had finally caught up with him, making such notions of order and discipline quaint and unimportant. *No more tomorrows for you, Captain Judah.*

For some time, Judah considered the quarters around him, long a place of refuge from his horrid memories and responsibilities.

His eyes wandered about the books and sheaves of paper on the shelves that had long made up his pained existence. A sad smile crossed his lips, and he experienced a moment of nostalgia, something that was an uncommon emotion in his tortured life.

He walked to the mirror on his wardrobe and stopped to gaze into his sunken eyes and booze-induced red complexion. Trying to make himself presentable, he patted his hair and tried to tamp down the uncontrolled whiskers in his unkempt beard.

Turning around, Judah saw his footlocker. Sighing, he kneeled and opened its lock, rummaging among the personal items and yellowed parchments stacked inside. Coming to a clean wooden case, he lifted it out and moved to his desk.

It was a beautiful and polished pistol case, with its ornate wood shining in the low light. On the top, "To an Officer of Distinction on his Wedding Day" was carved in attractive calligraphy.

Judah paused, running his fingers over the engraved letters as he prepared himself for what came next. His jaw trembled as he collected his courage.

Distant grunting and barking noises came closer from outside, and Judah snapped back to his senses. Opening the box, he looked down at two revolvers laid out beautifully and polished to a high sheen. Struggling with trembling hands, he grasped the weapons and held them down to his side.

After several deep breaths, Judah walked to the painting on the wall, where Sarah looked down at him from happier times.

As he huffed in preparation, her imagined—or perhaps quite real—words broke through his fear. *"It is time, dear. Have you missed me? Come, now. We will be together; it has been a long wait."*

More tears spilled from his eyes, yet Judah managed to overcome his abject terror. Suddenly assertive, he paced to the entrance door and flung it open.

With a final and deep sigh, he strode into the night, holding out both revolvers toward the darkness. As he strode onto the parade grounds, numerous shadows rushed to embrace his silhouette on the open area.

Gunshots, struggles, and grunts of pain followed, and Judah was finally able to reunite with his Sarah.

Chapter 7

Breathing hard, Crook stumbled to a copse of trees that loomed in the night ahead. Loraine and the troopers were hidden there, crouched in the brush and branches amidst dark tree trunks.

Nayeli and Hakan were nowhere to be seen.

"They went to scout a path to the mountain," said Loraine, answering Crook's curious look.

As he caught his breath, Crook and the remaining soldiers glanced back to Fort Hollenbush. Their mortified faces stared upon complete devastation, as flames shot from behind the walls and smoke billowed from multiple points within. Distantly, the echo of demonic wails continued from deep inside the fort, but no devil was visible from their current vantage point.

Backlit by the pale night and burgeoning flames, the skyline was remote and eerie. The soldiers gulped in loss at the destruction of the structures and the people inside.

For some time, nobody said anything, and each man processed the death of friends and comrades. Their teary eyes reflected on the rampaging fire, and they scanned the destruction with a detached sense of mourning.

Abruptly, Nayeli emerged from the darkness behind them, staying remarkably quiet and crouch-walking amongst some bushes. Nodding, Crook moved to her.

With his mind reeling from recent events, Crook calculated the best possible direction of their next travel. He sighed and stared directly at Nayeli, looking for an answer. "Does Hakan know the best route to proceed to the burial ground? We must choose carefully how we journey from this point forward. One mistake, and our fate is sealed."

Crook gestured back to the burning fort with a flick of his head, indicating their destiny if they didn't choose wisely.

Nayeli nodded, motioning to the darkness from where she just emerged. "It take several hours to get to the best point for deciding, Crook. But we must go now, before Chindi knows we escape."

Crook considered her answer, first looking at his men, and then to the dark shrubs that dotted the hilly starlit landscape to the west. Before he could agree, Loraine crept close and crouched near Nayeli.

"Lieutenant, we just lost our friends, home…everything," whispered Loraine, biting back his sorrow. "Now you want to follow the Indians, who can snuff the rest of us out? Is that smart?"

Nayeli didn't seem bothered by the accusation, but neither was she intimidated. "All of us will die if we wait, Crook. You decide where we go, but we must go now."

From far ahead, the screech of a bird came from another set of trees. Nayeli nodded toward it, looking concerned. "It is Father. He says the way is clear."

Moving his gaze between Nayeli and Loraine, Crook decided quickly, nodding toward Hakan's bird call with a frown. "Sergeant, get the men moving. We depart in two minutes. Don't let them think about our losses, let them think of our flight from this cursed place. If we stop, we are as dead as the rest."

Looking doubtful, Loraine nodded and spun to the other soldiers. As he moved off, Crook peered again at Nayeli. In the dim moonlight, an appreciative look crossed her intense features, then quickly melted away.

#

Under the cloudless night sky, the worn dirt path was remarkably well lit. The trail climbed between boulders and sparse trees as it ascended to a higher elevation, and the group trudged quietly in a single line.

The dusty ground around them had little plant cover, and puffs of dirt filled the air with each plodding step.

Motioning for the group to stop, Crook squatted behind a large rock to the side of the trail. Squinting into the moonlight, he struggled to see deeper into the night. Frustrated with the depth of his vision, he shook his head, as the view was not expansive.

The rest of the party behind also crouched behind cover, watching the elevated canyon cautiously.

Ahead, the trail split, with one path to the left moving up the mountain, while the one to the right dipped down into the murky foliage of a forested valley.

Crook shifted his gaze between the two options, unsure of which was better. Motioning for Hakan to move up, Crook leaned close to the chief when Hakan settled next to him.

They talked quietly for some time, with each moving his arms and gesturing to either of the paths forward.

After the hushed conversation, Crook and Hakan crept back and motioned for the rest of the companions to gather around him. Everyone crowded together, leaning close with shocked and fearful expressions.

"There are two directions we can take," Crook said. "The one over the mountain is the most direct route, and it will bring us more quickly to the burial ground."

Crook appeared doubtful and pointed to the path on the right. "Otherwise, we can go to around to the north, which will take longer but should provide more plentiful occasions to hide. I would appreciate your opinions on the matter."

Loraine spat to the side and spoke slowly, ensuring his words would be convincing and clear. "We'll have nowhere to hide if we go to the left. There's only brush and rocks on that mountain. If we get caught in the open, they'll kill us like hunted rabbits."

Hakan leaned in, staring first at Crook, then to Nayeli in some kind of silent confirmation. "It is good to go by mountain, Crook. My people avoid white man here many times. We call it Lone Mountain, a place of refuge for the Hewisidawi."

Loraine spat again, growing hostile toward Hakan. "How many times are you gonna let them lead us, Lieutenant? Until there's none of us left? What has your alliance with the chief brought to us, besides death?"

Crook didn't answer and instead looked to the others for input.

All but Nayeli were quiet, and she gave Loraine an irritated glance. "Chindi and his demons will not need rest. We must make large distance between them, but we must rest first, away from their evil eyes."

Crook nodded but balanced his gaze between the soldiers and Indians. His determined glance moved to Hakan. "How will we do that, Chief Hakan? We can't hide or rest behind the boulders up there. They will make quick work of us."

Hakan peered at each party member as he considered the discussion, eventually stopping on Loraine. Not flinching from the sergeant's acid stare, he gestured toward the path leading up the mountain's ridge.

"Up there, it is easy for us to hide, we have done so for long time. You will see our secret," Hakan said, and he suddenly stood up.

Stepping away from the party, Hakan nodded to Nayeli in order that she should join him. He moved several feet away from the soldiers, tucking his hands into his sleeves.

"We leave you to discuss, Crook. But do not take long time. Chindi will not be patient to find us," Hakan said.

With that, Hakan and Nayeli turned and walked into the night, moving toward the boulders and path on the left—their choice already made.

As Crook turned back to his men, Loraine got to the point. "Lieutenant, we're being played with…toyed with, like a cat with a field mouse. I can feel it. No disrespect, intended, but I've survived several wars by going with my gut. My gut's tellin' me to get the hell away from the chief. He's gonna be the death of us all."

Trumain, Blenchley, and O'Rourke nodded quietly, but their eyes were timid, flitting back and forth between Crook and Loraine.

"Fair enough, Sergeant. I heard your words—and your concern," replied Crook, keeping his voice calm. "But tell me: How is the chief responsible for any of this? If he wanted to destroy us, why did he not marshal his warriors to annihilate us when we came to his village? And why is he bringing his daughter among us if he intends to harm us? Your feelings are not rooted in fact."

Frowning, Loraine shook his head and pointed ahead. "I don't know what's going on, Lieutenant Crook, or what's happened, or what will happen. Demons, monsters, hellish creatures, whatever they are, I only know they're connected to the chief."

"He has admitted as much, Sergeant. His own people are being attacked—you have fought them in their wretched state. What else do you need to know? You among all soldiers know the dictum 'The enemy of my enemy is my friend.'"

Loraine stewed in his doubts for a while as conflicting emotions tugged at his grave expression. Unsure of himself, his thoughts ranged between wanting to pummel Crook to reluctantly agreeing to the chief's course of action.

Sighing, Loraine finally nodded, but his eyes weren't persuaded. "All right, Lieutenant, we'll do it your way," said Loraine, but his hardened features showed another unspoken message: *For now, Crook, but you're running out of opportunities to make choices that might get us killed—officer or not.*

Crook detected Loraine's dangerous skepticism and considered options to appease the man. Offering an unconvincing smile, Crook motioned up the path on the sparse mountain trail, where Nayeli waited next to Hakan in the faint darkness.

"Sergeant, we are only strong if we stand together against this menace, whatever it is," Crook said. "Without your efforts, we have little chance of enduring this fight. Your skills will be essential in the tasks we face."

Loraine spat a final time, then frowned at Crook. Standing, he quietly hiked up the trail toward Nayeli and Hakan. Crook and the privates soon followed him.

The chief and his daughter were relieved as Loraine approached, but Loraine offered them no greeting or smile as he passed by.

Hakan nodded at Loraine, but his gesture of appreciation was unreturned by the focused and now-belligerent sergeant.

The privates trailed in Loraine's wake, but their uncertain gazes moved back and forth between Crook and Loraine as they made their way ahead. It was as if they didn't know who was in charge—or even who should be.

#

Morning light illuminated Crook's face, highlighting the tired lines of his haggard features. Dust clung to his whiskers in smudged and chaotic patterns, making him appear crazy in a wild-man-of-the-forest way. As if to accentuate that look, Crook grinned broadly.

Staring over to Loraine, Crook's smile grew even more pronounced.

Shaking his head in response, Loraine shrugged back at Crook, and his expression was no longer defiant. He even allowed a partial grin to lighten his dour mood.

Around them, the rest of the group also smiled, taking turns looking exhilarated in the pale morning shadows.

They stood on a trail that tracked its way up a grade, with a steep cliff dropping off to the side.

Far below was a river, and the distant crash of water resounded up from its swift pools and rapids. Stunted trees stuck out from the cliff face above and below the trail, offering a scraggly and primitive appearance to the otherwise intimidating precipice.

To the side of the path, the rock wall was similarly sheer, with occasional boulders clumped together at intervals near its rough face. In the middle of the rocky wall, the sharp lines of a rough-hewn cave were visible, and a covering boulder was rolled out of the way to allow entrance to the mountainside. Hakan stood next to the opening, and even his serious face appeared amused.

"That is incredible, Chief Hakan," said Crook, gesturing to the rock wall. "How did you find such a place, and in such an isolated setting?"

Hakan motioned to the surrounding canyon, nodding with pride. He raised his voice, as if giving a speech. "Our ancestors have made this place for us. There are many such caves they use for many lifetimes, to keep food and for shelter in times of conflict. But none are as valuable as this. I show you this to show you can trust us."

Loraine rolled his eyes but stayed silent, while Crook frowned at him to keep quiet.

Hakan nodded to the cave opening, and Nayeli crouched and retrieved a crude torch and flint from inside the dark entrance. After several strikes, she set the wood alight.

With a faint smile to Crook, Nayeli leaned down and shimmied through the man-sized opening.

Hakan motioned for Crook to follow, but he stayed in his current position, inserting his hands back into his sleeves.

"After all go in, I will close behind you," Hakan said. "I see you soon."

Crook was perplexed, and he shook his head in confusion. After a moment, he shrugged and focused on the cave portal, where light from Nayeli's torch receded into the darkness beyond.

Inhaling deeply, Crook hunched down and followed Nayeli. Behind him, Loraine was the next to enter, followed by the rest of the troopers.

As Crook squinted ahead, he struggled to catch up to Nayeli, bringing himself close behind her. She was barely visible in the dim glow of the torch fire, but Crook's eyes focused down on her shapely form beneath her buckskin dress. His stare lingered there, and he banged his head on a low-hanging rock due to his inattention in the tight passageway.

Ahead, Nayeli emerged from the passage, and her light illuminated a large cavern. Crook stumbled out behind her, rubbing his head from his encounter with the dense rock. Nayeli smiled mischievously, amused at Crook's wound, as well as the reason for it.

As the other companions emerged into the wide room, its usefulness became apparent. It was an expansive cave, with enough space to shelter a small army—or a large tribe.

Various areas had wood stacked near fire pits to allow for cooking fires, and animal-skin bags stored large amounts of food staples. To the back of the cave was a shallow pool, with the already-sufficient water supply being fed by dripping from somewhere in the darkness.

Elsewhere, the stone surface of the cavern was covered by a sheen of condensation that reflected from Nayeli's torchlight.

Loraine whistled in soft amazement, staring around the cavern. "I've never seen anything like it."

"Yeah, it's like the coal mines in Virginia," said Trumain, appearing awkward and confused. "Except, there's no coal here."

O'Rourke and Blenchley chuckled in response as they scanned the huge cavern, taking in its enormous size and eerie shadows.

Still smiling, Nayeli spoke loud enough for all to hear. "There is place farther in cave to be used as a privy, but area is not so private."

Crook found himself blushing, so that even in the partial firelight, his embarrassment was obvious. He gestured for Loraine to get the men arranged for their stay.

As the soldiers clattered about with their gear and camp preparation, Nayeli approached Crook. Pointing toward an area to the back of the cave, she smiled. "Crook, come with me, I show you best part of our secret."

She moved to the back of the cavern, where she lit several more torches and placed them in crude sconces on the wall. Crouching carefully, she came to another crawl hole in a dark corner under the flickering torchlight.

Motioning again to Crook, she hunched down and squeezed into the opening, leading the way into the black and constricted passageway.

Outside, Hakan leaned into the large boulder next to the cave entrance. He pushed it with a grunt, and it neatly rolled to block the cave entrance again.

Reaching into some brush, he took out several branches and smoothed over the ground where the companions passed. Having covered their tracks, Hakan moved brush around the rock to make it appear entirely a part of the sheer cliffside.

After the cave entrance was camouflaged, Hakan stood still and waited.

Inside, Nayeli pressed her way through the passage. After some time spent shuffling through the darkness up an inclined rock path, she emerged onto a sheltered ledge above the trail.

From there, the path below and the entire canyon were visible, presenting a perfect view for people hiding inside the cave to watch for attackers. Reaching behind a rock, she grabbed a coil of sturdy rope and dropped it into the daylight.

Below, the rope unfurled and landed next to Hakan.

As Hakan deftly climbed hand-over-hand for forty feet upward, Crook stuck his head from the passage. Astonished, he stared over the entirety of the trail below, realizing he would notice any enemy pursuing them for miles away from their hidden spot.

When Hakan hauled himself onto the ledge, he pulled the rope up behind him, and his powerful frame showed no fatigue from the climb. He settled in a cross-legged pose and looked upon the remarkable scenery of the unspoiled valley below.

"Chief, this is incredible," said Crook. "With proper supplies, you could stay here for months and never give away your position. It is now obvious why we could never track you down for the theft of those horses."

Hakan shook his head grimly, gesturing to the path below. "Those horses were taken by outlaws from another tribe. But I knew you would not listen to us until I proved it. It is good you accept their scalps as payment."

Crook smiled distantly, clapping Hakan on the shoulder and continuing his gaze over the captivating valley. A moment of camaraderie passed between the leaders, and whatever their past troubles, they didn't feel far apart as people for the moment.

Moving carefully, Hakan reached over and took the white-beaded necklace from around his daughter's neck. Nayeli peered at her father, confused at Hakan's actions but still contented to enjoy the expansive view below them.

Smiling, Hakan put the Native necklace around his own neck.

#

A small fire burned in the central pit of the cavern. Sitting on a rock, Hakan stared into the flickering flame, lost in his thoughts. The temperature was brisk, and Nayeli huddled at his side, pulling a blanket tight for warmth.

In the background, the soldiers cleaned their weapons and washed their clothing in the area at the back of the shadowy cave.

Walking around in their long johns in front of Nayeli didn't embarrass them in the current state of the now-bizarre world, and they hung various items of wet clothing on a laundry line strung across the chamber.

As the soldiers hung up their uniforms for drying, Crook waded into the pool and splashed himself with the cold water, flinching at its freezing intensity.

As he washed himself, Nayeli watched him from the corner of her eye, trying to be subtle in appraising his form and conditioning. Crook didn't notice her attention as he scrubbed the accumulated dust of the trail from his body and hair.

Emerging from the pool, Crook shivered and padded over to the fire, where he sat across from Hakan and Nayeli.

Producing a straight razor, he leaned into the firelight, carefully shaving his whiskers while holding a small mirror. It was a difficult task to trim away errant facial hair in such a setting, but Crook's practiced hands did so in a precise manner.

Nayeli watched the effort with some fascination, intrigued as Crook scraped his face with the sharp blade. Her eyes studied each careful flick of the sharp edge.

Awakening from a daydream, Hakan noticed Nayeli's interest in Crook and offered her a disapproving glare, but Nayeli returned the look with a defiant stare.

Hakan shrugged at his daughter's fierce sense of independence, something he had long been accustomed to. Not wanting to incur the further wrath of Nayeli, he produced a pouch of seeds, which he scooped into his mouth and chewed absently.

"Crook, is it not difficult to arrange your face hair like that?" asked Nayeli. "Can you not just take it all away?"

Chuckling, Crook finished up his personal shave, closing the straight razor and tucking it into a pocket of his underclothing.

"I sometimes wonder if that would be a better option, but it is something of a fashion and statement of authority that a gentleman keeps a pronounced beard in current times," replied Crook.

Perplexed, Hakan shook his head.

"White man have too many strange customs. The Indian is fortunate to avoid facial hair games. We have not so much to worry about," Hakan said, pointing to his own whiskerless face.

Smiling, Crook produced a small can of wax, applying a small portion to keep his beard and mustache in proper order. "The truth is, Chief, throughout history it has usually been the case that military men were shaved clean, much like your people. Fashions are a fickle thing in the world, especially in our modern times of the telegraph and photograph."

Looking confused, Nayeli sat up. "How do you know how men shaved in the past, Crook? Did they draw pictures for you from long ago?"

"Most of what we know comes from writing, Nayeli," replied Crook. "But we have some paintings to show us how people looked in those distant times."

Hakan gave Crook a doubtful look, trying to work out the mechanics of what Crook was saying. "If you write down what happened, does language change over time? And if the person writing down what happened does not agree with others, how can you know it was correct?"

Surprised, Crook thought for a while on the question.

"I would suppose, Chief Hakan, that it would be presumed to be more accurate to have someone who was there at that time write about what happened...in order for details to be relayed more closely to their original state."

Hakan shook his head, apparently thinking Crook was too smart to believe what he was saying. "Our people pass down our history in stories. Each important word is made in our memory and agreed upon, then given to next generation like one before. This way, we know every word is real, every fact happen like we say. Nobody will be confused by crazy words from writing dead man from long ago."

Crook pondered Hakan's words. He moved to say something, but he stopped, reconsidering his thoughts. After a while, he shrugged noncommittally. "I never thought about it that way, Chief, but what you say has a certain logic to it."

Looking smug, the chief went quiet and returned his gaze to the flames. Nayeli smiled at her father, proud of Hakan's debating skills.

Loraine approached Crook from behind, leaning close. "Lieutenant, I'll take the first watch. Get some rest. We never know when we'll have the time again."

Crook considered whether to sleep first, then reluctantly agreed to Loraine's suggestion. Standing up, he nodded a respectful goodnight and walked to his bedroll in a dark corner of the cavern.

In that area, Crook arranged his meager personal possessions near his small bag. Checking his revolver, he placed it within easy reach, then lay down.

Settling in, Crook lay there for many minutes, turning over several times to adjust to the contours of the hard ground. Finally finding the right position, he inhaled softly and let his eyes close.

Abruptly, Nayeli slid into his grasp, nuzzling up to him under his sparse blanket to keep warm. She faced away from Crook, pulling his arm over herself and quickly falling into slumber. Her face was peaceful and unashamed, while Crook's panicked eyes didn't know what to do.

In time, Crook's face grew less worried, eventually becoming more comfortable with the warmer arrangement. A contented smile crossed his lips, and he joined her in sleep.

#

The afternoon sun beamed down on the crossroads of the two trails below the mountain. With no clouds to block sunlight, the day was clear and open. An energetic breeze swept across the remote setting, offering its low howl as company to the isolated backdrop.

Chindi stood at the point where the path split. Moving his head in his bizarre sniffing motion, he focused to either side of the trail, gazing back and forth with his dead eyes.

His gray skin was striated with black veins in the light of day, and his matted and blood-encrusted beard gave him the accurate appearance of a bizarre and hateful fiend.

Behind him, Chindi's burgeoning army was stretched out along the highland trail. Natives and soldiers alike stood in a hellish, otherworldly stupor, scanning the ridgelines and meager vegetation around them for potential prey.

Finishing his bizarre deliberations, Chindi motioned with both arms to the paths ahead. Heeding his inaudible orders, the group of devilish followers split into two groups, with a party of equal size proceeding on each of the trails.

As they trudged past Chindi, his cloudy white eyes watched them carefully, like a demonic shepherd admiring his despicable flock. When they had all passed him by, Chindi stood still for several moments, swaying gently and crooking his neck to either side.

Moving quickly, Chindi paced ahead, deciding on the path to the right. With wooden-like movements, he angled away from the mountain and into the darker woods below, where half of his abominable creatures had already descended.

Neither of his wicked groups looked back as they advanced along their routes, moving with certainty toward their distant and malignant purpose.

#

The cavern was quiet, except for occasional snores coming from the clumps of companions sleeping on the cold stone floor. Dim light flickered from a few torches on the wall, providing little illumination in the confines of the area.

A dark figure hurried across the floor and reached down to shake Crook. Opening his eyes, Crook looked up into the agitated face of Trumain.

Deeply disturbed, Trumain whispered as calmly as he could, trying to avoid awaking the others nearby. "Lieutenant, coming up the trail," said Trumain, and he motioned to the passageway leading up to the sheltered ledge above the cavern.

Nodding with glassy, unfocused eyes, Crook managed to disentangle himself from Nayeli without waking her.

Stumbling up, Crook grabbed his coat from the laundry line before ducking into the tunnel behind Trumain. While Crook scooted up the passageway, he came fully awake, and as his awareness returned, so did his fear of what he would see at the top.

When they crawled from the tunnel, Crook and Trumain perched above the trail, gazing into the early night and keeping themselves hidden.

The sky was overcast but well-lit from the moon's luminescent effect on the clouds, and it looked almost apocalyptic in its raw beauty.

Crook's breath caught in his throat as he stared below.

Strung out on the path were twenty-five of Chindi's demons, and they were making a good pace as they approached Crook's observation point.

The pestilent group numbered both Natives and soldiers, many of which Crook knew as friends in their former lives. They walked quickly, but their strides were mechanical, as if stepping too long a distance each time they extended a leg. Their heads swiveled as they walked, fully aware and scouring the area for victims. Crook and Trumain could only stare in dread as they approached.

The devils passed slowly below, their feet padding against the earth and rock. Fortunately, they didn't notice their quiet observers above as they moved by on the mountain trail.

Except, near the end of the demonic pack, one member stopped. With his head lulling in an odd search, Hollis stared up at Crook and Trumain. His wicked eyes and boil-marked skin seemed to radiate in the murky light. Hollis shouldn't have been able to see them, but he still focused on their elevated position.

As Crook peered down at the former corporal, an imagined message entered his mind from that putrid face: *You left me, Lieutenant. Left me to die, taken to hell by my own mother. And you call yourself an officer? You're a pathetic coward.*

Crook struggled to maintain his composure as Hollis continued his vengeful stare. Looking down at Hollis' blackened and desiccated hands, Crook saw he clasped a stuffed toy. Covered with blood, it was the doll of Hollis' young female cousin, the same that Crook retrieved from the destroyed stagecoach and that Loraine had left in his quarters at the fort.

Overcome with guilt, Crook put his face in his hands. To his side, the scared Trumain did the same, and they held their breath for what seemed an eternity as they prayed to remain hidden.

When Crook finally looked back up, his former friend and silent tormentor was gone, along with the rest of the creatures. The trail below was now empty.

When he glanced over to Trumain, Crook saw the same emotion on the younger man's face that he himself felt: crushing sadness.

\#

The sounds of the morning routine echoed through the cave, and each companion focused on their preparations for the day.

The soldiers finished donning their newly cleaned uniforms and checking their weapons, while Nayeli and Hakan packed stored food supplies into several leather satchels. Each person worked diligently, but the lack of conversation showed a sour mood permeating the cavern.

After the muskets were cleaned and balanced against the dark rock of the cave wall, the troopers gathered around the smoldering fire, joining Hakan and Nayeli. After they sat, Loraine handed each a pouch of dried berries and some jerky, along with a steaming cup of coffee.

Privates Trumain, Blenchley, and O'Rourke dug into their breakfast, chewing silently as they stared into the fire. Behind, Loraine patted each on the shoulder in a sign of protective attention.

After Crook accepted his food, he nodded appreciatively to Loraine and raised his voice, addressing the entire party. Nobody else appeared eager to talk.

"So, it would seem there are more of the wretches to deal with, as Chindi was not with this group of demons," Crook said. "It is essential that we avoid all his various bands on our way to the burial area."

Loraine nodded down from his standing position. His chaw of tobacco seemed to be his only breakfast. "Yeah, we gotta exit soon if we are to get there; it's a long walk."

Nobody was thrilled at the prospect of leaving the safety of the cave.

Hakan spoke to that point, appearing doubtful in the faint light. "We should give devils more time to get away from mountain. It is still dangerous."

Loraine grunted sarcastically, motioning to Nayeli and Hakan. "I've been in this region for three years, and it's never been anything but dangerous. To any of us. In fact, just about everyone I ever knew here is now dead, or worse."

The privates' nods at the sergeant made obvious their agreement with Loraine's opinion. They glanced slowly between Loraine and the Natives, awaiting a reply.

Crook shot Loraine a warning glance, while Hakan merely shook his head and stared forward. Nayeli appeared lost in her thoughts, not responding at all to the provocation.

"The white man was never invited to stay here in our land. He is an invader, not a friend," Hakan said, and he cast a wilting look of disapproval at Loraine.

Agitated, the troopers glanced around the fire. Their eyes were provoked and confrontational, so that even Crook's stern focus didn't cow them. Loraine went so far as to fix his openly defiant glare on Crook.

"We are here to keep the peace, Chief," Crook said, trying to appear moderate. "I've always treated you with respect."

Hakan nodded stoically and looked around the fire to the hostile glares of the soldiers. "That is true, Crook," But this is not your land—"

"I've heard enough of your horseshit, Chief," interrupted Loraine. "I've always heard it said by Indians that nobody owns the land. Now that others are here, you own it all? And what about your tribal neighbors? Not one winter passes without you killing each other in some raid. Is this your or their land?"

As one, the younger soldiers nodded their heads in agreement. Their eyes flashed a desire for revenge, wherever it could come from—and even if it was only to be verbal payback.

Crook held out his hands to calm the party, just as Nayeli snapped out of her daydream.

"It can always be true," Nayeli said, "that when fox steals the eggs of the bird, other foxes will never listen to the bird's complaint."

Crook stood up, moving close to Loraine and forcing a commanding edge into his voice. "I would have you all know that we are on the same side in this endeavor, whatever our history or personal feelings. If we have any intention of surviving this demonic plague, let us not turn on one another."

Loraine met Crook's eyes directly, then motioned to Nayeli. "I see only one person turning on his own, Lieutenant."

Crook took a long, deep breath, trying to control himself. He smiled at Loraine, but there was no mirth in his icy stare. Their surrounding companions traded glances in the flickering light, afraid of what would happen next.

"Sergeant Loraine, I have never met a more competent and professional NCO in my career than you," Crook said, sounding oddly clinical in his evaluation of Loraine.

Crook gestured around the fire to the other troopers, staring at each individually. "And I have never had the pleasure of serving with more hardy and committed soldiers than yourselves. You men have always done your duty with distinction and diligence, and it is an honor to command such a group."

Crook looked back to Loraine, and the sergeant's expression grew softer. Surprisingly, Loraine was the first to look away in their war of stares.

"I simply ask that everyone show some understanding at the particulars of our situation," Crook continued, "for all of our sakes."

Unexpectedly, Loraine spoke up, returning his challenging gaze to Crook. "Lieutenant Crook, I can say without reservation that you are the most honorable officer I've ever served under. And my time with the army goes back more than twenty years. I've served with all kinds, from incompetent bastards to drunken louts."

Crook was surprised at the compliment, and he remained expectantly quiet as he focused on Loraine.

"But we have watched all our friends and comrades be swallowed by this...Hell on earth," said Loraine. "So, I'm not inclined to listen to the chief's lectures—about anything."

Nods of agreement came from Blenchley and Trumain, but O'Rourke was somewhat unsure as he chewed on his jerky.

Crook considered Loraine's words for a few moments, dropping his head in concentration. When he looked back up, he nodded in feigned agreement, then pointed to Private O'Rourke.

"Private O'Rourke's father came to this country only two decades ago, correct?" asked Crook.

O'Rourke nodded, uncertain where the conversation was going.

"Because his family fled starvation in their home country, Ireland," Crook said. "Do you think it a lecture if O'Rourke complains about such a travesty of justice?"

Silence all around, and the soldiers pondered Crook's words with considered reflection. Even Hakan and Nayeli appeared contemplative.

"Right, so it is perhaps understandable that the chief is upset over what he has seen in his lifetime?" Crook asked.

Crook faced around the fire, looking at the entire group as he raised his voice.

"This does not mean that the world will return to its former situation, or that the chief's people can commit violence at will," Crook said, looking at Hakan with empathy. "But it does mean that he has a point of view that needs to be heard."

Unconvinced, Loraine scowled, but the tension in the cave deflated as the younger troopers returned their subdued gazes to the fire.

Without a word, Loraine spun and walked near the dark pool, where he resumed packing their equipment. Crook frowned at the back of the unhappy sergeant as Loraine shoved supplies into various bags.

"Now, let us ready ourselves for the journey ahead. We must find a way to stop...whatever this is from continuing to happen," Crook said. "It may be that the whole world depends on us to destroy this menace before it becomes even more dangerous."

The companions returned to their breakfasts, ruminating over the tense conversation and chatting in hushed tones.

Forcing a pleasant smile to his face, Crook paced back to the corner of the cavern to gather his things.

Rummaging among his few possessions, he stuffed them into a small pack. Closing the bag, he rolled up his bedroll with practiced ease, leaning his weight down to tie it into a compact bundle.

From behind, a hesitant hand reached down to touch his shoulder, and Crook looked back in surprise.

Nayeli stood above him, peering down with appreciative eyes. Dropping her hand from Crook's arm, she continued her kind stare, and for a moment they were both occupied with the same worry of what would happen in the unusual party's near future.

#

From the ledge above their hideout, Hakan stared into the cloudy morning, scanning the wide valley with a worried look. No sign of life was evident in the nooks and crags of the forbidding mountain, and a chilly wind blew with a lonely howl across its barren rocks.

Directly below, some large boulders blocked an absolute view of the ascending path directly under them, but there was currently no movement on the trail in front of the hideout.

To Hakan's side was Nayeli, and she matched his concern as she scoured the area around the mountain cave for any danger.

Hesitantly, Nayeli held up a long stick and dropped it from the ledge, where it clattered into the rocks near the trail below.

Nodding to Nayeli, Hakan unfurled the coil of rope and also dropped it down. With admirable agility, he lowered himself down the rope, making little noise as he let himself fall to the ground.

Hakan walked toward the stick but hesitated, then changed his course to step near the edge of the trail. Looking over the sharp cliff, his mind was preoccupied, and his thoughts turned inward as he peered down the precipitous drop. Awash with conflicting emotions, he considered their precarious situation as they faced an unknown future.

A short whistle from Nayeli brought Hakan's attention back to the present, and he glanced up to his daughter. She gave him a look as if to say *hurry up*, and Hakan nodded with a reproved grimace.

Hakan fetched the thick stick Nayeli dropped and walked to the boulder covering the cave entrance. With some considerable effort, he jammed the wood under the rock and heaved. After a moment, the boulder rolled from its spot, exposing the tunnel again.

Hakan glanced back up to Nayeli, and she smiled in appreciation. She pulled the length of rope back up, and after wrapping it in a coil, placed it to the side for future use. With an accomplished feeling and nod toward her father, she disappeared back into the upper tunnel.

Hakan set aside the wooden prying tool and returned to his vista point, staring distantly over the pristine valley. He concentrated on pools of water in the river below, following the current as it flowed over rocks and shrubs, forever replaying its ancient cycle. His eyes misted over as he imagined his ancestors watching the same natural wonders of this cherished and wild landscape.

Behind him, a scraping came from the cave, and Blenchley poked his head out. As his eyes adjusted to the streaming daylight, he nodded warmly at Hakan and grinned.

Feeling suddenly freer in the morning sun, Blenchley stood and strode toward Hakan. Smiling, he was glad to be out of their dark and constricting hiding spot.

The crack of a pistol shot resounded on the rock walls near the trail, and Blenchley was thrown forward, where he landed helplessly on his knees. In his back was a severe bullet wound, and blood pumped freely from the jagged hole.

From the dark corner of the wall, where the boulder met the shadows, stepped the possessed Hollis. The devil moved into the light, holding a revolver out and scanning the area with its abominable white eyes. Moving ahead, Hollis focused down on the wounded trooper, pointing its weapon.

To the side, Loraine scrambled from the passageway, eyes alarmed and searching for the source of the gunfire. Seeing the demonic Hollis, Loraine yanked a Bowie knife from his waist scabbard and flipped it expertly into a fighting grip.

Spinning toward Loraine, the creature cocked the hammer and pulled the trigger, but only a click answered its efforts. The demon did so again and again, but each attempt at shooting Loraine ended with the same empty result.

Seeing his chance, Loraine screamed a battle cry and rushed Hollis. Plowing into the demon with jolting force, they thudded into the rock wall. Ramming his knife into Hollis's chest, Loraine leaned into the pommel to drive the blade through the fiend's despicable heart.

The tip of the vicious blade barely pierced Hollis' gray and cracked skin. The demon's white eyes stared directly into Loraine determined features from inches away, and its fetid exhalation was like a blast of vile sulfur.

As Loraine grunted with his efforts to impale Hollis, the demon flipped around his revolver, grabbing it barrel-first. With a brutal smack, Hollis brained Loraine with his empty pistol, sending him spinning into a nearby boulder, where Loraine slid to the ground with a defeated grunt.

Trumain leaned out of the mountain cave, rushing to pull out his musket behind him. The demon saw the incoming threat and moved quickly toward the exposed soldier.

Another pistol shot boomed from the side, as Hakan held up one of Crook's personal revolvers and carefully aimed at the demon. Walking slowly toward Hollis, he fired again and again as he got closer.

Most of the bullets struck Hollis to little effect, but one hit the demon in the cheek, blowing a hole through the taut skin and exposing the off-white cheek bone. Black liquid leaked from the wound as Hollis turned to face the chief.

The dreadful Hollis stared at Hakan, seemingly unsure of what to do. His head lulled in demonic indecision, as if searching for the source of the new attacks.

The boom of Trumain's musket was deafening in the contained area. The front half of Hollis's head disappeared in a black mist of gore and skull fragments, and the creature slumped against the wall as the contents of its skull painted the rocks behind it.

Trumain held out his smoking musket, looking undecided and scared as his gaze moved from the destroyed Hollis to the other members of the group.

Crook moved next out the passage, holding up his own weapon and scanning with a confused expression for a target.

Noticing Loraine first, Crook rushed quickly to the sergeant, who struggled to rise from where he had been thrown. Blood poured over his face from a head wound, but Loraine's eyes were fully aware.

Coming to his senses, Loraine motioned over to the injured Blenchley.

"Blenchley," shouted Loraine, and he stumbled over to the wounded man. Blenchley still crouched on his knees, looking confused and peering around while he wheezed in an effort to draw air into his ruined lungs.

Crook hurried over to comfort Blenchley, leaning down to speak to his face. On his other side, Loraine tried to staunch the flow of blood from the grave wound to his back.

"You'll be all right, Private," said Crook. "I've been injured several times, and…"

Loraine met Crook's gaze and shook his head, just as Crook's words trailed off.

Groaning in pain, Blenchley spoke in a terrified voice, trying to arrange his words in proper order, even as his perceptions of the physical world drained away with the same speed as his pumping blood. "I'll be up in a minute, Lieutenant. I just need to catch my…"

A spurt of blood surged from Blenchley's mouth, coloring his lips and chin with a bloody foam.

Blenchley's eyes were scared, and they searched Crook's face for relief from his severe pain. Looking toward the sky, they became unfocused as he uttered an unintelligible prayer.

Focusing on the sun, Blenchley's eyes locked open, and he slumped into Crook's arms.

Nayeli and O'Rourke came next from the cave's passage and hurried to the tragic scene. Each moved their eyes around, not knowing what to do as they peered down, terrified at the sight of the dead trooper in Crook's arms.

Crook and Loraine held tight to Blenchley, holding him in an awkward death embrace. As they eased him to the ground, silence and sorrow filled the air.

Taking note of Loraine's headwound, Crook pulled out a handkerchief and held it to Loraine's head. Loraine nodded appreciatively and used the cloth to soak up the blood leaking from his scalp.

Collecting himself, Loraine pulled out some loose bandages and tied them around his head. As the cloth turned red, Loraine cinched them tight with a pained grimace.

Trying to think through his pain, Loraine grew confused. Walking over to Hollis's corpse, he stared at it, studying the creature from inches away.

"How did it know to wait here for us?" Loraine asked, growing suspicious.

Loraine pointed to Hakan, confusion filling his pained face below his bandaged head. "And why did it not attack Hakan when he was the first to come out?"

Hakan looked both confused and disturbed as he glanced over to Hollis's remains, then back to Loraine. "This is big problem. Only Chindi should know when we are near. These devils should not know this..."

Hakan shifted his eyes between Loraine and Crook several times, then focused completely on the lieutenant, as if Crook might have the answer for what just happened.

Crook shook his head in response, searching his memories for a clue to what led to Hollis' attack. "I don't think so, Chief. I saw this creature marching up the trail, and he knew I was on the ledge. He could not see me, I think, but he knew it nevertheless."

Crook ran his hand over his mustache and beard, tamping them down in a nervous gesture. "I think these devils keep a portion of who they were in their current state. Somehow, they are more than mindless denizens from hell. In the future, we should be very careful in supposing we know everything about them."

Loraine didn't look convinced, and he stared over at Blenchley's corpse, then back to Crook.

"I think there's more to this than we're being led to believe, Lieutenant," said Loraine, and he stalked around the trail, looking at the prior night's tracks from the demonic group.

Loraine moved his gaze up the rising trail, where the tracks led. Up there, the path crested the mountain in a few hundred yards and was lost as it snaked down the opposite ridge. With his inquisitive bearing, Loraine looked like a hunting dog on the scent of prey, despite his bloodied head and makeshift bandage.

"And I am going to find the truth behind all of our men's deaths," said Loraine. "Even if I have to go to Hell itself for the answers."

With that, Loraine grabbed the legs of Hollis, dragging the revolting corpse toward the cave.

"And I'll never leave another of my men to be picked clean by buzzards," Loraine said, grunting as he pulled the corporal's legs. "They've earned the right to be laid to rest—in the chief's cave, at least."

As Loraine yanked the hideous form of Hollis into the darkness, Crook nodded in agreement. Gesturing to O'Rourke, he grabbed the feet of Blenchley, and together they carried the recently killed soldier into the passage behind Loraine.

The remaining party watched them go in, staring hopelessly at the latest victim of their foul adversaries.

Chapter 8

It was evening in the forest, and a biting wind blew through the trees. Rustling branches swayed under the wind's onslaught, moving in coordinated rhythm over a broad area of woods and brush.

The movement of the trees' leaves and needles created a strange Fwhooshing, sounding something like the flow of distant raging water.

Through this turbulent area the party struggled on, looking ahead and squinting, as if they'd been caught in the middle of a raucous and uncontrolled sea.

The companions leaned against the gale, pulling cloaks and animal skins tight around their cold bodies as they pressed through the swirling forest. As a group, they were chilled and miserable, with icy stares and clenched jaws.

In the lead, Crook stopped for a moment and fumbled inside his pack. Pulling out a compass, he stared down and held it against a fluttering map. Glancing around, he tried to get his bearing, but his puzzled look wasn't a good sign for him knowing their precise location in the frigid wilderness.

Crook raised his voice to be heard in the whirling trees. He wasn't overly confident in his words as he panned his eyes about the woods. "This is Burney Meadows, where they found a settler dead several years ago, I think. It is good land, but the elevation is not conducive to an amenable temperature."

Loraine moved near Crook, leaning over the map and looking closely at its contours. Being as uncertain of their exact location as Crook, his mood soured at their surroundings.

Gathering his breath, Loraine spoke in a bitter tone. "Burney was killed by Indians, butchered like a hog at his homestead. The man never had a chance—just another murdered innocent."

Frowning, Hakan walked carefully past Crook and Loraine. He avoided looking at Loraine, evidently not wanting to discuss the matter.

Staring ahead into the darkening woods, Hakan scanned the shadows carefully. Collecting himself, he spoke in a non-apologetic voice. "There are good and bad men in all tribes," Hakan muttered. "Why are the bad Indian men here my fault?"

Hakan looked pointedly back at Loraine, not hiding his sudden contempt for him. He spat his words out, fighting numbness from the cold as he talked. "And why the bad men in your much larger tribe not your fault?"

Crook lowered his map and compass, putting them roughly away as he moved between Loraine and Hakan. Trying to get Loraine's attention, he gave the sergeant a reprimanding glare.

Loraine avoided Crook's stare, but he met Hakan's surly eyes without flinching. "That's a good point, Chief. Unless you're one of the bad men we're talking about."

"That's enough, Sergeant," Crook said, holding his hands up in a sign for him to calm himself. "We are all on the same side here."

Loraine frowned at Crook and Hakan, shaking his head with unhidden doubt. Sighing, he stepped around the pair and plodded into the shadows, letting Crook know exactly what he thought about being on the same side.

Continuing ahead, the Natives proceeded after Loraine. As Nayeli passed by Crook, she offered him a sympathetic frown and patted him on the shoulder.

Coming next, Hakan did the same, nodding amiably as he strode after his daughter.

Not appearing reassured by the gestures, Crook looked back to his remaining soldiers with a frustrated scowl.

#

The bad weather and freezing wind continued, and now it was fully night. Frost hung from trees in the high mountain forest, and snow covered the ground in patches near dim clusters of brush ahead.

The already poor visibility was made worse by a mist hovering over the dark forest floor.

Crouching, Loraine squinted back in the darkness at Crook. They could see and make out each other's features in the moonlight, but not much was clear beyond that.

"There's a large building ahead," said Loraine, and he cautiously scanned their near surroundings. "It's some kinda farm with a few outbuildings around it. There's smoke coming from the chimney."

Crook was surprised at the revelation, and he arched an eyebrow as he focused into the night's shadows.

"I was unaware that the area had been reoccupied," Crook whispered, taking care to avoid too-loud noises or speech. "Who would take the risk to build in such a primitive area? No one would ever be safe in such a far-removed location."

Loraine didn't answer, offering only a worried stare to answer Crook. The only sound from the other party members came from chilled hands being rubbed to keep warm.

Trumain was the first to speak up, sounding whiny but getting to the point. "Lieutenant Crook, it's as cold as hell, and I can barely feel my feet. Maybe we could see if they have some free space for us to bed down inside?"

Crook thought for a moment, then nodded hopefully. Creeping forward through several stands of trees, he stopped near a partial clearing in the murky landscape. At the periphery of his vision stood a farmstead, and it was precisely as Loraine described.

It looked strangely peaceful amidst the shadows of the dark woods, and light shone out through several of its windows. Two storage sheds and an outhouse lay next to the building, and a small, dark barn was situated to the back of the structure.

Crook moved silently back to the party, leaning down and keeping his voice low. "It would be a good idea to seek shelter in the home, if the residents are hospitable to strangers. I will go first, and—"

Ignoring Crook, Loraine stood and walked brazenly through the brush, pacing toward the quiet home. He made no effort to conceal his movements as he blustered toward the building.

Sighing, Crook gestured to the others, and they readily followed behind him.

#

The small home was lit by several lamps, keeping its wood-lined confines bright and comfortable. A robust fire burned in a hearth at the back of the living area, ensuring a cozy and warm living space, while a door on the rear wall marked the entrance to the only bedroom at the back of the house.

Henry Clayton sat on a large handmade chair near the flames. He held a large Bible in his hands, reading carefully in the firelight with an intense and interested look on his kindly face. In his forties, he was a homely man with a bald head and thick glasses, but his features were also pleasant and kind.

In the kitchen area abutting the living room was his wife, Bonnie, who scrubbed at a pot in a simple sink. Of similar age to her husband, she was rotund and hardworking, and she wore clothes that were fit for a life of toil and hands-on labor. She whistled softly as she attacked the dirty pan.

Next to Bonnie was her daughter, Sara, who was old enough to just be in school but not likely to have that opportunity in their current location. Sara cleaned several dishes with a rag, and a stack of sparkling cups and plates sitting on the counter indicated her proficiency at her work.

In the rest of the room were multiple pieces of basic but sturdy furniture, from a large table and chairs in the kitchen to several wardrobes braced against two of the walls.

Because of this isolated area, the furniture could only have been made from Henry's own carpentry skills. The shiny condition of the various pieces, as well as the cleanliness of the rest of the room, was testament to the family's fastidious work.

On the wall were a multitude of Christian crosses, spaced every few feet. The largest hung above the fire, with the enormous crucifix announcing in no uncertain terms the faith of the home's occupants.

At other places on the log walls and in picture frames on top of furniture were paintings of the Virgin Mary and Jesus Christ. All were kept free of dust and matched well with the religious motif of the environment, offering a comforting backdrop to the simple frontier home.

Henry gently shut the enormous Bible and raised his voice to Bonnie. "I do believe there is another family moving into the old ranch at Jack Rabbit's flat. They are named Arnold and Edna Haley, I believe. What a wonderful addition to this area they will make, and they even have a child that could be friends with Sara. We shall have to visit them with dinner, I think. They could surely use our help in fixing their home, especially with winter bearing down on the Meadows."

Bonnie turned around, wiping off her hands with a white towel. Her pleasant face smiled in ready agreement, with her extensive wrinkles highlighting her arduous life.

"Agreed, Henry, but the traveling preacher said last month that they were Mormons. Hope they don't mind Catholic neighbors."

Henry beamed an illuminating smile towards his wife, one that could have lit the room all by itself. His crooked teeth made his face no less pleasant.

"If we have to wait for other Catholics to come here, we'll never have the chance to make friends, Sweet Bonnie," Henry said, motioning out the window. "Besides, if the Lord can forgive me all my weaknesses, we surely can forgive them for not seeing the world like we do."

Bonnie merely smiled and nodded, matching the intensity of her husband's kind features. To her side, Sara set down her cleaning rag, turning around with a sheepish grin.

"Father, would you mind if—"

She was cut off by three firm knocks on the door.

Standing, Henry looked curiously at his wife and daughter. He stared at the door with a concerned expression. "Who on earth could that be out at this hour? I hope no one is in trouble."

Walking to the corner of the room, Henry grabbed and lifted a shotgun that was balanced against the rough wood. He approached the front door carefully, glancing worriedly at his concerned family. "Who is it?"

From the door's other side, Crook's chilled voiced answered. "Sorry to bother you, but I am Lieutenant Crook, from the US Army. I was hoping you could let us in, in order to get out of the cold for a while. Your help would be abundantly appreciated."

Surprised, Henry lowered his gun and promptly unbarred the door. Opening it, he stared out in surprise at an intriguing sight: four soldiers and two Indians, distraught and very cold.

Henry's kind voice could not have been more appreciated, even if it came from heaven itself. "Well, don't just stand out there freezing. Come in and get warm."

#

The party sat around the large wooden table, looking intensely at bowls of thick soup. Plates of bread also filled the table, making the various members fixate on the succulent food—and their hunger. Steam rose above the table from the bubbly concoctions, serving as a smoke signal for the companions' eager taste buds. Even the mellow Hakan licked his lips in quiet anticipation of the beef stew and fresh bread.

By the fire, Henry and Bonnie stood beaming at the party. Sara peeked her head out from behind her father's leg, looking shy but interested in the strange visitors.

"Please, eat," Bonnie implored them, and she clasped her hands together, eager to watch their unusual guests enjoy her hardy meal. "You all look famished."

Crook nodded to the group, and they abandoned all manners as they dug into the meal. With nods and grunts, some more polite than others, they slurped down the food.

Loraine, abandoning his normal aversion to excess eating, looked like he was going to cram a whole loaf of bread down his throat as he gnawed on the end of a recently dipped crust.

For some time, the feast continued. The members focused on the meal like it was made for a king, and from the looks of their satisfaction, experienced it the same way.

As the grunting and chewing continued, Henry spoke up in a friendly voice. "I can't say that I've ever seen such a sight. How on God's earth did such a group of people find its way to my door? It is good that you found us in such foul weather."

Chewing slower in a passing attempt at manners, Crook glanced above the hearth to the large Crucifix. The figure of the crucified Jesus seemed to look down at him, making him nervous as he considered his next words.

After the staring contest between God and man lasted a few moments, Crook conceded defeat and returned his serious gaze to his gracious hosts. "This is perhaps the best stew and bread I have ever had the joy of eating, Mr. and Mrs. Clayton. I do propose that you folks are a gift from God, helping us like you are."

The other companions nodded in agreement but still avoided talking as they continued their meal. Contented smacking accompanied their flitting eyes as they monitored the conversation while gorging themselves.

Henry and Bonnie smiled widely, and his mention of God didn't hurt the intended impact of Crook's compliment.

Crook's voice turned less happy after he swallowed his last bite of stew. Bracing his arms on the table, his manner grew serious as he collected his thoughts.

"We are from Fort Hollenbush," Crook said glumly, looking sadly at the rest of his travelers. "It lies...about forty miles to the east, over the mountain. We do not come here with pleasant news."

Henry peered quizzically at Crook, and he tightened his lips in a worried expression. Glancing briefly at his wife, he stared again on Crook. "Lieutenant, what brings you so far over here, to Burney Meadows? I hope you're not here over troubling matters. Or violence? We've found this area to be most hospitable for our intentions."

Crook looked to the soldiers and Natives around the table, and his expression assumed the air of an official death announcement.

Crook's companions stopped chewing as they were forced to consider their precarious situation, as well as that of their new hosts, and the joy of the tasty meal faded away.

Henry, Bonnie, and even Sara responded by growing more worried. They stared at Crook, then to the others in the quiet room. As the silence continued, their expressions filled with deathly expectation.

"I will tell you everything, Mr. and Mrs. Clayton," Crook said, his eyes growing grave. "And not just because of your hospitality...but for reasons of common decency, because I have information you will surely wish to act on."

#

The room was quiet, and the soldiers stood in an arc around the fire, leaning close to it for warmth. Each had a sober and serious expression as they gazed at Bonnie and Henry Clayton in the flickering firelight.

Sitting at the table, Nayeli and Hakan were also occupied by the seriousness of the situation. They frowned as their eyes moved back and forth between the troopers and their hosts. Steaming mugs of coffee lay on the table in front of them, untouched for the moment.

"You're saying there are actually demons on earth? Physically...here?" asked Henry. "And they've destroyed your fort? I hope this isn't a joke? I've never had the appreciation for such humor."

Crook nodded, trying to balance his emotions about losing his command with the need to save further lives.

"I wish it were not so, but that is how we are here," answered Crook, and he nodded over to the scared Sara. "Most important for your sake, it is good that we came upon you when we did."

Breathing deep, Crook slowly paced the room, stopping to look about the cozy home and taking in each of the crosses and paintings. He let his demeanor become thoughtful and deliberate as he took each step.

"I do not know from where these devils emerged," Crook said, appearing almost used to the idea of living demons. "But they are certainly here and killing...or turning...anyone who comes into their path."

Bonnie, distressed and worried, glanced to her daughter. She half-whimpered as she talked. "How is this possible? How does the Lord allow such things to happen?"

From the table, Hakan cleared his throat. "This is an evil spirit from long ago. It has returned for me and all people that get in its way. It will not stop until it kills or takes everything...or everyone."

Henry stared skeptically at Hakan, but he avoided saying anything negative out of politeness.

Noticing his reluctance to believe, Hakan addressed Henry's doubtful look. "The Great Spirit talks to all his people. But to each in his own language."

Thinking a moment, Henry tilted his head in agreement to Hakan's reasoning. Glancing again at Bonnie, he assumed a hopeful expression, like the chief's words were wisdom itself.

"I think you are right, Chief Hakan," replied Henry. "Our good Lord has many rooms in his mansion, and I don't see why he would see fit to only speak in one language."

Hakan smiled grimly, his eyes focusing on the couple. "But the devil also speaks in different tongues. So, this enemy is but one face of evil. It came from old Indian spirit who wants to destroy everything."

Loraine, reserved and quiet up to this point, pointed over toward Sara. His tone was strong and serious as he shifted his gaze to her parents. "All of this is true, Mr. and Mrs. Clayton. In the morning, you must leave this area without hesitation. If they come for you here—"

Loraine gestured to the shotgun leaning against the wall, shaking his head at its futility.

"—you will not be saved from certain death, or worse."

Overwhelmed, Henry pondered the blunt warnings. Staring around at his visitors, he mulled over his options with a horrified but determined look. After a moment, he slowly shook his head. "The Lord has always protected us. We even have Native friends here in the valley."

Crook gently raised his voice, motioning to the area around the group with both arms. "This is not an evil of man, or something you can reason with. It is something you must avoid at all costs. If they come for you here, there will be nothing left. You and your family will die."

Nayeli stood and approached the Claytons. Her face was sincere and honest. "Chindi will come for you. You will be killed or become slave to him. You must take family away."

Crook walked behind Nayeli and placed his hand gently on her shoulder. It was an action that didn't go unnoticed by her father, who frowned from the table.

"Mr. Clayton, tomorrow we will travel to the Pit River to fight this demon," Crook said, and his determined expression pivoted around the room to meet his companions' gazes in a show of confidence. "And we will destroy this abomination, no matter the cost. In the meantime, please go west before the snows trap you in. In the spring, you can return, and it will be safe again."

Henry's jaw hardened as he stared about his home, searching the faces of his guests. Considering their warnings, he nodded kindly, but his eyes were single-minded in his faith.

"I appreciate your concern, I truly do. But we trust in the Lord for everything, from our food to our protection. He always rewards those that believe in him, and it's my intention to make our home in this valley. If the devil himself comes here to stop us, it is God that will stand with us."

Henry's gaze moved to Hakan, and the chief stared inquiringly at the religious man, wondering if he was enlightened or simply stupid. The chief shook his head, sadly dropping his gaze from Henry's stubborn eyes.

The rest of the party was deflated, and they peered at the small family as if they were already dead. It suddenly was harder to look at the three with the knowledge they could soon become Chindi's next victims.

Sighing deeply but trying to remain respectful, Crook let go of Nayeli and moved to the fire near his men. He motioned to the untucked uniform shirt of Trumain, which the soldier quickly fixed.

"I understand, Mr. Clayton," said Crook, accepting Henry's decision reluctantly. "Would it be agreeable to you if we stay the night? We shall make no further requests on your hospitality."

Bonnie nodded vigorously, but her worried gaze drifted to her daughter as she motioned graciously to the wood floor.

"Yes, of course, you are welcome to stay for as long as you need. And I will make sure you travel with full stomachs when you depart.

We'll keep the fire burning so the chill doesn't reach you during the night. The weather turns colder with each day."

The group smiled in response, nodding thankfully at the kind couple and their deep hospitality.

Crook gestured for the party to make preparations for sleep. As each of the group unrolled their bedroll and unpacked personal items, they glanced worriedly at their hosts.

#

A morning mist crept across the sparse field, blocking the outlines of trees that stood in blurry shapes behind a dense wall of morning fog.

Birds chattered in staccato rhythm from the surrounding forest in the daylight, lending a pleasant background to the rustling of breeze-assisted branches.

Crook stood in the quiet field bordering the back of the house, looking thoughtfully into the dense foliage. With his hands perched on his hips, he listened and watched, straining his ears while squinting through the cloudy tendrils of morning haze.

Satisfied, Crook turned from the forest and walked back to the Clayton's home. In the daylight it was even cozier than before, with rough-hewn logs and carefully crafted windows offering a folksy and rustic atmosphere.

On the porch stood the Clayton family, who nodded and smiled at their soon-to-depart guests.

Off to the side, Loraine got the privates ready by checking their packs and murmuring in low conversation. The men nodded back at him and chuckled as they got mentally prepared for their upcoming travel. With the pleasant day raising their spirits, their path ahead seemed for the moment a bit less strenuous and worrisome.

Nayeli and Hakan stood back from the Claytons, looking respectfully up at their hosts. Hakan was as calm and still as a frozen statue, while Nayeli smiled and waved at the always-happy Sara.

In response, the young girl bashfully returned the wave while holding onto her mother's hand.

Keeping a pleasant demeanor, Crook approached Henry, who gazed down with his permanently optimistic expression. Extending his hand to the religious homesteader, the lieutenant offered a genuine and heartfelt smile.

Henry clasped his hand in a firm shake, one that surprised Crook with its firmness.

"Mr. Clayton, I would be immensely happy if you would depart the area until this horrible turn of events is over," Crook said, keeping his voice low. "You will have many years to reclaim your home and prosper later. It is not an area that you will need to worry about excessive competition from other settlers."

Henry smiled but didn't answer Crook's suggestion. Instead, he caught Crook off guard. "Lieutenant Crook, are you a man of faith?"

Crook's kind look wilted, and he was forced to collect himself, as if he had been asked a loaded question. "I...believe in God, Mr.

Clayton, but I don't worship as perhaps I should. Life has not made faith the easiest option for me."

Henry nodded and motioned toward Loraine, who still chatted with his men. "I imagined it would be so. A life that forces a man to lead a path of violence and toil can make faith in God seem quaint."

Crook was surprised at Henry's intelligent assessment, and he eyed the humble man with new interest. "Umm, yes, that has been a hindrance in the past. But I have also found that the idealism of religion can limit one's capacity for dealing with critical situations. Generally speaking, of course."

Henry took a step down from the porch, coming out of earshot of his family and leaning closer to Crook. "But I expect you try to live honorably in life and your profession. Right, Crook? My intuition tells me you're an honorable man?"

Crook flinched ever so slightly from the verbal onslaught, almost taking a step back. "I...try to live well, Mr. Clayton. Society requires good men to do so; otherwise, we have only chaos. The bad in society will always win if not confronted by men of good conscience."

Henry nodded, agreeing quietly. He glanced to either side, noting Crook's assorted companions with a kind assessment.

"So, we truly serve the same God, Lieutenant, just in different ways. Just like the chief and his daughter, in their own capacities."

Crook thought over Henry's words, but he appeared unable to respond.

Henry continued his unexpected and insightful appraisal of Crook and his companions. "As for your desire for me to leave this area, it's not an easy choice to make. What is faith for if it is only to be disregarded in the moment when life becomes difficult? Am I to live my faith, or flee like a child before this evil demon that stalks our real world? Would Christ flee from his tormentor, even as he was ordered to be strung up on the cross?"

Taking a considered breath, Crook shook his head in disagreement. "It doesn't take faith to realize your unwinnable situation, Mr. Clayton. Life is full of simple compromises one must make to protect oneself—as well as one's loved ones."

Crook gestured to Henry's family, and Henry responded with a loving stare at Bonnie and Sara. Grinning faintly, his thoughts were elsewhere.

"I would also offer that you are not Christ," Crook said, and he punctuated the statement with a stern, finishing glare, as if the debate was won and over.

Henry answered the challenge with a thoughtful nod. "True, Lieutenant, I am a flawed and horrible sinner, let there be no doubt about that. But he did order us to be like him, in all ways. Is that not so?"

Sighing, Crook shrugged and gave up the discussion. Like a gambler who finally knew when to give up on a game, he extended his hand to Henry in a show of a reluctant goodbye.

Nodding politely, Henry shook heartily and moved to the porch, where he surveyed the departing party with an honest grin. Bonnie and Sara joined him in offering a happy sendoff to the weary party, even though a bit of nervousness remained under their pronounced smiles.

Crook moved toward his men, where he inspected their kit and preparedness for the trail ahead.

As Crook checked their weapons and equipment, Nayeli abruptly walked to the porch, where she began a final chat with the Claytons. By the time Crook completed the inspection, he was forced to wait for Nayeli's still-unheard conversation to finish.

When Nayeli finally returned to the assembled group, both Crook and Hakan looked at her inquiringly. In response, she shrugged and walked into the misty forest, ignoring their unspoken questions.

As the rest of the party followed her, Crook took a last look behind, waving sadly at the Claytons. When he turned forward, Loraine stepped next to him, matching his pace.

"Hell of a shame; they seem like the nicest people," said Loraine. "But you tried, Lieutenant. That's all any of us can do in the end— our best."

Crook reluctantly nodded. "That may be true, Sergeant Loraine, but their young daughter does not get the luxury to choose. Why is Mr. Clayton so unrelentingly stubborn?"

To this, Loraine chuckled and shook his head. Letting himself fall behind Crook, Loraine looked over Trumain and O'Rourke's equipment as they marched. He continued his exasperated chuckles as Crook trudged ahead.

Left alone, Crook suddenly appeared bewildered as he walked. Pivoting his head around, he looked confused and self-conscious. "Sergeant, what did I say wrong?"

#

Evening descended over the extensive orchard, causing discolored clouds to take on an orange-red glow in what remained of daylight.

Below the clouds, rows of trees offered their own-colored variety of blooming, presenting a multitoned and radiant spectrum of foliage at the end of the autumn day.

Among a stretch of apple trees, Hakan and Nayeli were hunched on their knees, staring out over lower-lying fields that led to a small river. The current in the flowing rapids was mild, but the water was deep. Silent, they exchanged mesmerized glances as they considered the attractive scenery ahead.

Crook approached them from behind and squatted next to Hakan, peering across the river with an interested gaze. Looking closer, he focused on the rippling river and frost-tinted fields that led up to it.

"As I understand it, this is not the river we seek?" asked Crook, rubbing his hands together for warmth. "We should have considerably more time to travel?"

Hakan smiled faintly. "No, Crook, it is some way to go before we are there. But it is good time to stop, for rest overnight."

Agreeing with a nod, Crook settled into the expansive overwatch position next to the Natives. Getting Loraine's attention behind, Crook indicated it was time to camp for the night with a circular motion of his fingers.

Loraine nodded and hustled back to Trumain and O'Rourke.

As Crook squinted into the darkening sky, Nayeli silently attracted her father's notice with an exaggerated stare from her wide-open eyes.

Hakan was confused for a moment, but he soon scowled as he caught Nayeli's intent for him to get lost. When her eyes sharpened, appearing like she was going to physically harm him, Hakan reluctantly agreed to the non-verbal suggestion.

"Crook, I go to prepare fire with soldiers," Hakan said, and he hurried away from the bluff, shaking his head and murmuring "*crazy daughter*" in his native language, Achumawi.

Crook noticed the strangeness of his departure, but he was clueless about the reason why. He shrugged as he resumed his peaceful stare into the waning daylight.

"Crook, why are you not married?" asked Nayeli, and she moved her dark eyes directly to his. They were beautiful, and Crook suddenly noted their ravenous intent as she focused on him.

Nervous, Crook tried to talk, then stumbled like a tongue-tied teen as a blush moved across his whiskered cheeks. His voice cracked several times as he tried to appear normal.

"Nayeli, I...err never had the opportunity to marry. It is difficult to find a woman who would be willing to adapt to this military life. My life, in any case."

Nayeli looked doubtful, tilting her head in confusion.

"You have no women around you to marry?" asked Nayeli, growing suspicious. "You around men all time? Live only with men? Maybe you like men for...?"

Nayeli made a pounding-fist movement with her hands.

Crook's face turned crimson red, and he actually choked for a moment as he shook his head. "No, I assure you, never that. I...am merely waiting for the proper woman to make my wife."

Crook's face continued to flush as he returned his gaze to the river.

Nayeli nodded, staring intently at the befuddled officer. Reaching out, she touched his knee, and her grip was not unpleasant.

"I have decided I want you, Crook. I will be your wife," Nayeli said, growing serious. "We will join tribes, a chance for peace between the Hewisidawi and white man. It will be good for our people—and us."

Crook's breath caught in his throat, and it appeared a heart attack was imminent. He glanced around, praying for Chindi to interrupt his exposure to actual feelings.

"What about your father, Nayeli?" asked Crook, overcoming his shock and keeping his voice low. "What would he think of such thoughts?"

Nayeli looked annoyed, scrunching her face up and wondering how Crook could be so ignorant. "My father is good leader. He would be happy to lose daughter and gain ally. He also likes you, but thinks you are like pappy sometimes."

Perplexed, Crook arched his eyebrow as he tried to understand. "Pappy? He thinks I am like a grandfather? Wise, you mean?"

Nayeli thought for a moment, struggling through her confusion as she looked for the right word. Understanding, she giggled momentarily at Crook's heightened sense of self-worth.

"No, Crook, you are like dog, young one that lives life without understanding real world," Nayeli explained, still searching her memory. "*Puppy*. I learned this language from nuns long ago; it is difficult to remember all things."

Disappointed, Crook moved his gaze back to his men, who chatted over a small fire. None of them looked interested in his love woes or marital aspirations.

Breathing deep, Crook turned back and met Nayeli's eyes. Now, some of his own wants, his desires from years of loneliness, bled into his words.

"Nayeli, I do not know if that is possible, even though it is an appealing proposition," Crook said, and his piercing expression showed he meant it. "These things can take time in my world— sometimes a year or more to arrange."

Nayeli nodded in a matter-of-fact manner, not concerned with Crook's responsibilities or planning troubles. She leaned very close to his face. "After we defeat Chindi, we marry, and you become friend to our world. You become...bridge to my people."

She leaned closer yet and gave Crook a long, wet kiss, then embraced him. In shock, Crook trembled like a cowering servant as he absorbed the kiss and hug. Being a man unaccustomed to physical contact, he was like malleable putty in Nayeli's masterful and artistic hands.

Nayeli pulled back a bit, her eyes intense and her skin flushed. "If not, then you can return to your man world, and life without me. And both our peoples lose a good future."

Crook melted under her gaze and didn't respond while he stared into her beautiful features. He wasn't categorically opposed to the idea of marriage, and his mind raced as he considered the possibilities and problems of such a union.

Crook also trembled at other thoughts taking root in his mind, ones that were of a decidedly less polite and more animalistic nature.

With an affectionate smile and pat on his shoulder, Nayeli stood and walked to the campfire. Pleased with herself, she moved freely toward her father, like nothing of consequence had just happened.

Chapter 9

The lazy creek wasn't broad or deep as it rippled in the afternoon light. Its mild rapids splashed down over flat rocks into middling pools, creating a shimmering background under swirling eddies of mountain water. Around the stream were swaths of mangy grass and overgrown trees, flanked by large rocks and muddy soil.

Nicholas Haley stared into the pool from his position on a boulder near the shore, watching the line from his simple fishing pole make its way into the creek's depths. He was a strapping boy, dressed in long blue shorts and a matching vest. An open can lay next to him on the rock with a glob of slimy worms squirming inside it.

Nicholas chewed on his lip, focusing and trying to will a trout to take his drifting bait. For a considerable time, he waited for the fish strike he knew should be coming.

Nicholas' eyes dropped in disappointment when his desire for a fish went unanswered. He squinted into the depths below, trying to determine the exact whereabouts of the fish that should be stalking his lonely hook.

"It's OK, son, we already got several. We gonna feast tonight," said Arnold Haley.

Behind him, Nicholas's father had a friendly and comedic manner, one that matched his puffy, unkempt hair and crazy-looking eyes. His simple farm clothes were well worn but otherwise clean around his middle-aged frame.

Arnold stood on the muddy bank of the creek, holding up a stick that had three trout hanging from it. The stick acted as a stringer, with its point stuck through each of the fish's torn gills. Blood ran freely from the skewered trout, with the pointy branch dripping continuous dribbles of it to the ground below.

Nicholas pursed his lips and nodded, not hiding his sadness. "I wanted to catch big momma today. Mother wanted me to get that big fish we're always after. Said it'd be good luck if we get her this time."

Arnold smiled broadly as he took the fishing pole from Nicholas. He pointed to the trickling water as he bent down, peering into his son's big eyes.

"We'll get your 'big momma' fish another day, son," Arnold said. "We gotta leave the big ones sometimes. Otherwise, they don't make more that we can fry up later. Remember, it's better to catch one hundred of her small fishes than one of her."

Thinking a moment, Nicholas grinned, realizing he couldn't argue with his father's logic.

Smiling, Arnold motioned to a picnic lunch, and Nicholas collected some half-eaten sandwiches as Arnold packed up their fishing supplies.

After they were in proper order to walk home, they hiked down the shore of the creek, snaking their way through reeds and dense brush. As they pressed through the clogged shrubbery, they held up the pole and picnic bag to avoid entangling them in the constricting overgrowth.

For an hour, they forged through the thick weeds, until finally turning away from the gentle water toward an open field stretching some distance to the side of the creek.

In the distance of a green and plant-inundated meadow, a rough ranch home sat in isolation, awaiting their return. With log walls leaning at precarious angles and a tattered roof, it wasn't in great shape, but it was nevertheless homebase for the fishing duo.

The tired father and son plodded toward it, their feet quickening with each anticipatory step. Arnold eagerly grinned as he strode toward the homestead, and Nicholas was able to just match his father's pace, even as he required twice the steps to keep up with him.

As the house came into clearer view, something seemed out of place. Curious, Arnold stopped, putting his hand lightly on Nicholas's shoulder.

Standing still, they were confused as they scoured the open fields around them. The sound and setting seemed...strange, like nature itself was momentarily off.

Suspicious, Arnold cocked his head to get a better look at the back of the home. There, the clothesline in the backyard was out of its mooring. Drifting from it were a host of clothes, which fluttered and dragged in the light wind on the dirty ground.

Confused, Arnold took his son's hand and stepped gingerly around the side of the house. As the backyard came fully into view, so did the form of his wife, Edna Haley.

A plump woman, Edna stood next to the fluttering clothesline and its dirty apparel, staring at the back of their home. She was unmoving, seemingly locked in place, as she faced away from her husband and son.

"Edna?" asked Arnold, sounding worried as he glanced around. "What are ya doing? The clothes are getting filthy on the ground."

No answer came from his wife, and Edna continued her blank observance of the house's back wall without a response. Rigid and still, she made no move to turn and greet her family.

Meanwhile, a whoosh of sound picked up from the breeze on the grassy field to their backs. Except, the sound seemed louder than should have been expected from such a light wind.

Still holding his son's hand, Arnold stepped closer to his wife. As he moved within a few yards, he angled to the side, trying to get a view of her normally kind face. Leaning forward, he tilted his head, peering expectantly.

Behind Nicholas Arnold, a host of crawling shapes emerged from the tall grass, and the source of the excessive sound around them became clear. Moving in bizarre and shimmying pulls across the grass, the unwieldy devils pulled themselves free from the higher grass on the exterior fields surrounding the ranch home.

With their boil-covered skin and gray hands, the wretched figures of Chindi's creatures stood and sprinted toward the backs of the unaware father and son.

When Arnold was almost at a point to see Edna clearly, he jerked his head back toward the incoming danger, and his eyes went wide in terror.

A score of fetid and dark faces ran across the grass with outstretched arms and hungry, blank eyes. As they closed the distance, there was just enough time for Arnold to squeeze Nicholas's soft hand before the hideous demons leapt upon them.

#

The morning was cloudy in the meadow, and rolling shadows from dark clouds moved across the endless high-mountain prairie. Farther out, imposing mountains stared down on the remote area, offering a raw and intimidating backdrop for the incoming cold season.

Loraine stared down in disgust, a cloth held over his face. Across from him, Crook did the same as he exchanged distressed glances with the rest of the party. Everyone was silent as they tried to avoid retching, while an army of flies buzzed in a droning chorus in front of them.

Below them were several sheep and portions of other skeletons lumped together in a large natural ditch. Some remains looked like they were part of a large horse, while others were half-eaten portions of smaller creatures, including a coyote, various rabbits, and a mountain lion. Maggots infested the flesh and organs that remained in the rancid pile, while the white skeletons of other remains suggested they had been there for some time.

"What does it mean?" asked Loraine, and he looked to Hakan. "Chindi is eating whatever animal he encounters?"

Hakan shook his head, frustrated and unsure. "This is not something I know. Demons collect animals for some purpose."

"It's like it's an eating place for 'em," said Trumain, and he pointed down with a nauseated stare. "Looks like they come here to feed, and anything with meat is what's for supper."

Stretching his back, Crook stared across the field, squinting into the distance of hills and never-ending grasslands. Returning his gaze to the demonic food trough, he covered his mouth again. "Two matters concern me about this find. First, this means the devils require sustenance, or at least think they do, and they are not merely driven by an evil spirit for their ends."

O'Rourke chimed in, appearing interested while he peered down at the revolting mess. "Why does that surprise you, Lieutenant? Everything's gotta eat, including the possessed— whatever they are."

Crook nodded behind his handkerchief mask, and after a moment, he stepped back to escape the hideous death stench. He spoke louder as he pulled away the cloth. "That is true, Private, but it also makes them more dangerous, and our task that much more important. If they had run out of victims in this portion of

California, an area with an insubstantial population, we could at least have hoped that this pestilence would run its course and die away."

Nodding her understanding, Nayeli took her chance to speak up, motioning to the remains below. "But now they could continue spreading as far as sun. Until there are no food or people left to feed them."

Hakan seemed particularly bothered by the new information, and he reached for Nayeli in a show of concern. In turn, she rested her hand on his arm and smiled as she tried to console him.

Loraine snorted a sarcastic laugh, shaking his head in frustration. "More good news for what remains of our little army. Who could have imagined our situation could actually become worse?"

The group grew quiet, and Crook considered what the apparently new information meant for their already poor prospects for survival. Their odds didn't appear to be improving, and the stakes for people far beyond this remote locale had just increased substantially.

After a deep breath, Loraine spoke again. His voice was more controlled, and he sounded genuinely curious as he peered at Crook. "What is the second matter, Lieutenant? You said there were two things that concern you about this...food?"

Remembering himself, Crook nodded at Loraine and gestured to the pile of animals. "Yes, well, the second matter we need to consider is that there is a great deal of meat left for them, and I suspect they will soon be back for it. We should depart quickly, without rest or delay."

With that, the party lost no time in responding, and each member hurried to prepare for resuming their journey.

The soldiers gripped their muskets for a quick march, while the Natives faced into the morning light, focused and ready.

Showing no fatigue and plenty of motivation, the companions hurried on their way, attempting to put the vile site from their minds.

Across the putrid pile of rotting animals they left behind, the buzzing flies were left alone to continue their meal.

Chapter 10

Hakan righted himself, yanking on the strap of a leather bag that chafed his shoulder. His face was in its customary unemotional setting, and he looked at the cluttered tree line to the side of the path near the forest.

Raising his eyes, he wiped his brow with a colored rag. Moving his gaze from the sun, he glanced warily around the field the group was marching across. Located at the back of the line in the hiking party, he tilted his head, making mental calculations for their location.

"Crook, stop. We come close to burial place," Hakan said, and he continued to rotate his head as he made note of the landmarks around them. "We will be here for some time."

At the front of the small column, Crook stopped and looked back at the chief. He panned his gaze around, confused and searching. "Here?"

Hakan shook his head at Crook, as if the officer was a lost boy in the woods. Ahead of her father, Nayeli smiled at her father's obvious frustration with the Lieutenant.

"No, not here, Crook," said Hakan. "On other side of the woods, across river."

Confirming Crook's confusion, Loraine also moved his head about, searching for the reason they had stopped. "Why would we stop here, Chief?"

Hakan pointed to the thickets of trees next to the open field, where the sheltered interior of the forest had collapsed trunks and dead wood draped throughout its dark confines.

"We must make sharp sticks for weapons and for fire," Hakan said. "There will be good wood here."

Crook followed Hakan's gaze, and he surveyed the deep forest with a considered gaze. Nodding, he spoke to Loraine. "Sergeant Loraine, please have the men collect whatever wood the chief deems necessary for our endeavors."

Crook rotated his head, then pointed to another portion of the forest. "Also, collect larger portions of wood there in order to build several bonfires, as well as whatever we need to construct a raft. Do not wear yourselves out prematurely, but ensure we make haste. We don't know how long we have before our pursuers will visit us. We should feel lucky if we have a few days before they come."

Loraine looked suspiciously between Crook and Hakan. Agreeing with a shrug, he walked toward O'Rourke and Trumain, pointing to the wooded thickets.

"Let's get to work, privates. The sooner we start, the sooner we can either...die or kill these maggots."

The troopers didn't seem inspired by his words, and they each frowned. As Loraine got close, all three began taking off their thick military coats for the impending difficult work.

Taking a heavy drink from his canteen, Crook breathed deep and stripped off his own heavy officer's coat. Looking into the collection of timber, he walked to join the work detail, moving toward the shaded woods with a determined stride. As he paced ahead, he pulled a long knife from a sheath on his belt.

Completing the group effort, Hakan and Nayeli met eyes, and moving to join the soldiers in the overgrown trees, removed their own excess clothes and equipment on the way.

#

The interior of the woods was murky, only partially lit with errant rays of moonlight on the shadowed forest floor. Branches in the above canopy of trees shifted and rustled, creating uneven sounds as they swayed with a forceful breeze in the darkness.

A single figure stepped into a ray of dim light, its head moving curiously to evaluate the surrounding brush and trees. Its movement was not unfamiliar as it performed another odd sniffing gesture in the shadows.

Chindi stood still, waiting for his purpose to develop as his blank eyes panned through the dark environment. He scoured the periphery of the surrounding foliage, waiting as he always did— for his right time to move. As with all predators, his success at hunting required a keen and perceptive understanding of his environment and prey.

This demonic orchestrator of death and possession was not a force that moved on instinct alone, but instead thrived on calculated and effective intent. Unlike a predator of flesh that ran on spurious instinct, his efforts were in tune with an organized scheme of death and obliteration on an industrial scale.

Taking a step ahead, Chindi tilted his head and motioned it forward ever so slightly.

In answer, a flood of his devilish henchmen moved from behind him, streaming through the forest with halting precision. Largely quiet, they stepped around and through brush and trees as they pressed forward, single-minded in their aggressive and calculated movements.

At the edge of the woods, the retinue of devils stopped in perfect coordination. Shuffling in behind them, Chindi stared over the open meadow, where the Clayton house stood by itself in the shadowy night.

With another nod from Chindi, a lone figure stepped from the tree line. Slow at first, it grew faster as it padded across the clearing towards the humble structure. In the darkness, the home showed no internal light from its windows as the small figure approached.

The blue shorts and vest of Nicholas were just visible in the faint light of the moon, but splotches of dark liquid also covered portions of his clothing. Walking to the front door, Nicholas's gray arm reached up to knock.

The diminutive creature knocked with a sharp rap on the dense wood. When no answer came to the taps, he beat a firm series of further thumps on the door, spacing them out as they echoed throughout the lonely clearing.

With no response, Nicholas's unseen face waited. Tilting his shadowed head, the boy placed a mottled hand on the door and moved it over the wood, rubbing the coarse wood beneath his small bloody fingers and broken nails.

As if begging the occupants to emerge with the caress of the door, more time passed for the Claytons to meet their horrid visitors.

When nothing happened, devils suddenly surged from the surrounding forest, moving with speed as they scrambled toward the home.

As some creatures flooded to the front porch, others leapt through the glass windows of the house, crashing into the darkness beyond.

The tearing of furniture and doorframes followed, and as was described in Crook's warnings to the religious couple, the Claytons got a chance to host a new set of houseguests.

#

Grinning, Crook appeared contented as he stared to the side. Across from him, Loraine was also satisfied, and he nodded at Crook with a reserved smile.

Both men were covered in sweat and grime, and streaks of sap and bits of bark were embedded in their ragged clothes.

Trumain and O'Rourke stood breathless to the side, their shirts untucked and with circles of perspiration filling out their armpits.

Nayeli crossed her arms and peered ahead, also taking her time to catch her breath. Though fatigued, she gently smiled at Hakan. In response, her father offered her a mild grin, managing to briefly break free from his permanently stern mood.

Near the river were enormous piles of trees and branches, the result of the group's extensive efforts to collect wood.

The branches were stacked separately from the trunks and bound together by narrow strips of cloth, while the larger trunks were aligned and pointed at the river, as if prepared to be dragged across it.

A small recently built raft lay on the riverbank next to the assembled wood.

The river itself was large and beautiful as it gushed with raw power past their location. A series of shallow rapids flowed in the middle of the stretch of river, and to either side were large pools of churning water, ones that were both deep and forbidding in their wild state.

Across the river was a somber site: an extensive burial ground location with cairns and Native symbols hanging from them. Long-deceased skeletons clung to various burial structures throughout the area, and their open mouths and eye sockets seemed to cry out to the party, as if complaining about their odd condition in the brisk autumn day.

Crook's grin melted away as he scanned the bones of Natives and their grave markers. A universal aspect of military men, as well as with people in general, was a reluctance to tamper with the dead or to disrespect their final place of rest.

Hakan noticed Crook's misgivings and gave him a reassuring nod to allay his fears. Motioning to the remains that adorned the extensive Native cemetery, he raised his voice. "Crook, men that are here were the most honorable of my people, here for many generations, including my ancestors. They died as warriors, both young and old, whether in their sleep from old age or on end of spear. They still are here, watching over us. Waiting for us to join them."

Crook didn't appear eager at that prospect, and he shook his head slowly. "That may be the case, Chief. But let us keep from joining them too soon. We have a lot of wayward devils to send to them in the meantime. As an old military saying goes, 'The stars incline us, but they do not bind us.'"

The chief looked surprised for a moment, like he was amazed Crook's input could be enlightening. Smiling and nodding his agreement, Hakan reached to his neck, gently taking off his white-beaded necklace and placing it on Nayeli. Grinning, he patted her shoulder after it was in place.

Loraine watched the transfer of jewelry with a distant stare, his contemplative eyes turning over some unrealized memory as he peered at the Natives.

Turning to the rest of the group, Hakan spoke in a low and controlled voice. "From this point, we must be careful and respect the dead. Chindi will try to draw power from old spirits."

Nods came from the others as they faced toward the peaceful burial area. Each member scanned the quiet death poses of the long-deceased men, imagining themselves in their place. It was not a comforting thought for any of the troopers, perhaps not even for Nayeli, and their eyes flicked nervously from one skeleton to another.

The sounds of smooth water and gentle rapids became the only audible witnesses to the morbid scene, and the group fell into a contemplative and hypnotic state.

Abruptly, Hakan strode forward to the stacked wood, putting a hand on the bark of a long tree and rubbing it. Reaching into his tunic, he pulled an enormous knife from a hidden scabbard and stuck it into the wood, where its end vibrated from the force of his throw. The watching soldiers looked surprised, apparently not knowing the chief was ever armed with it.

"And our work has just begun," Hakan said, gesturing across the river. "We must be ready for Chindi and his demons, and we need fire and sharp sticks as best weapons against them. They will not wait long to find us now."

#

A day later, the group stood silently on the side of the river with the quiet burial ground. Each person's gaze swept around them, proud and exhausted. They appeared more fatigued than before, and all were filthy with grime and pieces of bark in their hair and clothes.

The burial side of the river had been completely remade. Facing toward the shallow rapids, two concentric barriers of spikes had been erected, created as rough fences with barbs and crude spears sticking in every direction.

Most of the sharp points extended toward the water, and their ends had notches down their lengths so that anything impaled on them would be unable to easily extricate itself.

Between the barriers was a narrow open area, one that faced directly at the only portion someone could easily cross the shallow water. It was a killing field, meant to draw in their heinous foes. Several stacks of tied sticks and branches lay near the opening, serving as a point to illuminate the area around it.

Across the river, more piles of collected wood lay ready to be set alight, and they were carefully sited to act as marker fires to illuminate any direction their attackers chose to cross the river.

Behind the fire and entry point, set thirty yards into the burial area, was a large barricade. It had open ports set throughout its branches, allowing for clear firing lanes on the river and its bank. On blankets behind the barricade were muskets, powder canisters, and homemade spears.

Hakan looked proudly over it all, happy with the trap and his companions' preparations. "Chindi will be drawn by spirits. Here we will slay him and his followers. None will escape us."

Hakan walked forward, pointing at the riverbank and the thickets of lethal fences. "When Chindi dies on this sacred ground, we bury him, and his devils return to their bad place. They will live in torment in spirit world."

Hakan glanced back, first to Nayeli, then at Crook. For the first time, Crook witnessed a genuine and boisterous smile cross his normally stoic face.

"And we will all be safe again," Hakan said, nodding eagerly.

Happy, Crook returned the smile and turned to his men. As he was about to speak, from behind came the distinctive click of a revolver being cocked.

Spinning around, Crook saw Loraine pointing his Colt revolver at Hakan's face. Loraine's features were grave, and his finger was almost touching the hair-trigger.

Behind Hakan, Nayeli was shocked. Her gaze jumped around, trying to figure out what was happening. She implored Crook with her shocked eyes to stop whatever Loraine was doing.

Loraine didn't flinch as he pointed the weapon precisely at Hakan's brooding face. The sergeant simmered with hatred, his finger drifting ever closer to the trigger.

Oddly, the chief didn't seem surprised at the turn of events, and he dropped his resigned gaze to the ground. Suddenly, he took on the appearance of one who, living constantly in a dangerous game, finally had to face up to his sins.

"Sergeant Loraine, what in God's name are you—?" yelled Crook.

Loraine quieted Crook with a taut finger held in warning. "Do you want to tell him, Chief, or should I?"

Loraine lowered the revolver to his waist, still keeping it pointed at Hakan. Trumain and O'Rourke, both as confused as Crook, glanced nervously at the unfolding drama.

"The chief has been playing us from both sides, Lieutenant Crook," Loraine said, speaking coldly. "He's been killing us this whole time."

Nayeli started to move forward, but Loraine turned his piercing eyes her way, stopping her cold. "I do not wish to shoot a woman, but if you interfere..."

Unsure what to do, Nayeli's hand crept close to the pistol tucked in her waist. Loraine smiled, shaking his head slowly, and the truth radiated from his deadly expression: *If you do it, you'll be dead before the barrel is raised.*

Nayeli moved her hand away from the weapon, still staring defiantly.

"Have you gone insane, Sergeant...Lorenzo?" Crook said, trying anything, including a name change, to slow the murderous intent in Loraine's face.

"Relax, Lieutenant Crook," said Loraine, lowering his voice to a steady tone. "It's the necklace he was wearing."

Loraine pointed to the necklace that now adorned Nayeli's neck. Crook's confusion persisted as he stared between Nayeli and Loraine.

"He uses the necklace to hide from Chindi," Loraine explained, moving his confident gaze to Hakan. "It has some kind of power."

Loraine stared at the chief, waiting for an answer. Hakan nodded reluctantly, slowly raising his eyes in acknowledgment.

"Yes, it keep Chindi from seeing me," Hakan replied. "Or knowing where I am. It come from old shaman in my village. For protection."

Irritated, Crook raised his voice, almost whining. "Why didn't you tell me this before, Chief?"

"Because he didn't want you to know the truth," Loraine said, stressing each word.

A look of realization crossed Crook's features. "You took the necklace off when you came to the fort. You gave it to Nayeli..."

"Exactly, Lieutenant. Which led Chindi and his demons into our midst, where they killed everyone," Loraine said, and he clenched his jaw in renewed hatred.

Nayeli shook her head, staring incredulously at Hakan. "This is not possible. Father...?"

"My daughter did not know, Crook. It was my decision. It is me to blame," Hakan said, looking sadly at the soldiers, one by one.

"I noticed something was wrong when Hollis killed Blenchley near the cave," Loraine said. "Why didn't he attack the chief instead, especially if Chindi wants his blood the most?"

Trumain stepped closer, clutching his musket with violent intent. "You killed all my friends?" Trumain asked. "Everyone...?"

Loraine nodded, smiling bitterly and warning off Trumain with an understanding glare. "Yes, he did. In cold blood, knowing we trusted him."

Exasperated, Crook rubbed his beard, as if wanting to pull it out by the roots. His eyes were stretched in disbelief. "I trusted you, Chief. How could you commit such evil?"

Hakan smiled without humor, raising his troubled eyes to Crook. "My people live in this area for fifty lifetimes," Hakan said. "We hunt. We fish. We make a good life—"

"You are a bastard, sir," interrupted Crook.

"But now, disease takes us," Hakan continued. "White man's disease. War takes us. Your fire water and promises of free food make us into nothing. We have no future in this world now. I had to...drive out the white devil with the real devil."

Loraine stepped close, pressing his revolver into Hakan's ribs. Nayeli looked at Crook, hopeless and fearful pleading in her eyes.

"You are going to die, Chief," Loraine said.

"I did what I had to, Crook," Hakan said, ignoring the sergeant, but there was no conviction in his eyes. "You are leader. You would protect your people—no matter what."

"I act with honor, Chief. Life without honor is not worth living, no matter the cost," Crook replied.

"Crook, honor means nothing if your people are dead...your lands lost. Your heritage, gone forever," Hakan said, and for the first time his voice took on a pleading manner, as if he felt he had to make Crook understand his murderous motivations.

The confrontation went quiet. Defeated, Crook peered down, looking for something—anything—to salvage the horrible predicament. He brooded for a long time, and only trickling water occupied the silence as the others waited.

When Crook looked back up, there was something new in his demeanor. Conviction flowed through his features as he faced Hakan with fierce and righteous eyes.

"Every evil man who ever lived claimed the same, Chief," Crook said, and he stared until Hakan looked away.

Crook raised his voice, motioning to the work they had done up to this point. His tone was restrained and mildly confident as his gaze swept over the party.

"The chief deserves to die for what he has done, of that there can be no doubt," Crook said, looking at everyone except Nayeli. His men nodded in an eager response, and their angry features filled with a desire for vengeance as they stared at the chief.

Crook faced Hakan again, this time leaning very close to his face. He stared intently for some time, watching the chief's eyes, like he was looking into his soul.

"But I will give you a choice to face this evil you have used against us," said Crook. "This abomination that has slain so many of my good men at your behest."

Looking down, Hakan responded slowly, with shame and anguish flowing under his expression.

"Thank you, Crook, it will be good honor for me to die a warrior's death, destroying this demon. I will avenge all the people he has taken."

Crook nodded, then gazed directly at Loraine. Admiration infused his voice. "And you saw through the ruse, Sergeant. In spite of everything, you have been right all along. We are lucky to have you, and I will never forget your sound judgment. Let us hope we live to fulfill your efforts at survival."

It was quiet as the companions absorbed the evolving events. Looking less angry, Loraine pulled the revolver from Hakan's ribs, and the chief was able to breathe easier.

"We will lure Chindi into our trap, and Hakan will be the bait. We will ambush and kill this hellish beast, ending this wretched plague for good," Crook said, his voice rich with hope and charisma. "When it is done, we will proceed to Fort Bidwell, where we will inform this country that death almost came for them all. Perhaps this will help stop the war that threatens to end our divided nation."

Crook focused on Hakan, his former respect for the chief replaced by a calculating glare. "How long do we have, Chief? Chindi knows we are here, correct?"

Hakan looked south, answering quickly and nodding. "Two days. No more, and only if we are lucky."

Loraine took Nayeli's revolver from her waist, tucking it into his belt. As he grabbed and began tying Hakan's hands, the chief looked into his eyes. "Thank you, Sergeant. Please...look after my daughter. She is good and will be a tool of peace for you. For both of our peoples."

Loraine didn't meet his gaze, instead glancing over to his fearful daughter. Nayeli peered back with dread and unending worry in her crestfallen features.

"I will do my best, Chief," said Loraine, lowering his voice so Nayeli couldn't hear. "Unlike you, I will give you and your people a chance. Remember that on your way to hell, because if there's any justice, that's where you're going."

#

Hakan sat cross-legged on the ground, staring intently into the fire. Around him, the night was illuminated by the moon, throwing its faint light across the burial ground in luminous rays. The creepy ambiance of the crumbling burial structures was sharpened by the pale glow highlighting the unmoving skeletons.

Hakan had an eagerness to his bearing, one that spoke to his desperate situation and recent experience. Unafraid of death himself, he still wasn't at peace with his actions. The only cure for his shame was to exorcise his own demons with the application of brutal violence.

It had been too long for a warrior like himself, and Hakan felt the driving need to drench the earth with the blood of his wicked enemy. He would find a way to vanquish the wicked Chindi and make the world right again.

Hakan licked his lips in anticipation. Glancing across the river, he scoured the signal fires for signs of the devils. Nothing was yet visible, but his time was coming. His appointment with destiny and the chance to meet his people in the spirit world was something Hakan craved, and it was a desire he soon expected to fulfill.

Behind Hakan, the barricade was barely visible in the extended light of the campfire. Behind its shadowed outline crouched Loraine, O'Rourke, and Trumain. They squatted low, holding their muskets and scanning the river and fires for signs of the incoming devils. To their side was Nayeli, who sat near the powder supplies and spare firearms, ready to assist in reloading as necessary.

For a considerable time, the group watched the flames and flowing river. The incessant trickle of the current was the only sound in the darkness, making the anticipation worse due to its peaceful and contradictory calmness. Such a relaxing environment did not mesh well with the death and evil that were surely coming their way.

Hakan suddenly focused to his left. A single figure rushed across the signal fire and quickly disappeared into the upstream pool. Even farther up the upstream shoreline, another series of figures were backlit by another firelight as they rushed into the river. Their various outlines disappeared under the river's dark surface, gone into its frigid depths without hesitation or concern.

Behind the barricade, Loraine leaned close to Nayeli and the privates, whispering in hushed expectation. "Stand ready; they're here."

More vague outlines crossed to the south of the rapids, rushing into the downstream churning water. Only mild splashes accompanied their movement under the gently roiling surface.

Trembling with excitement, Hakan glanced to his side. A cache of several homemade spears lay next to him, waiting to be used against the noxious creatures. Grabbing one, Hakan rose to his feet, balancing the weapon with practiced ease in his weathered hands. The lines of his worn face glowed in expectation, and Hakan felt as one with his ancestors.

"Come to me," Hakan whispered, panning his head about as he searched for his enemies.

A head emerged from the water, followed by a demon running onto the shore, angling toward the pointed pickets.

The boom of a musket matched with half of its head disappearing, and the creature slumped to the muddy bank, sprawled awkwardly with its limbs at odd angles.

Behind the barricade, Loraine nodded to Trumain and O'Rourke, passing his smoking weapon back to Nayeli for a reload. He pointed out toward his handiwork. "Make your shots count. Get 'em in the head or neck."

Five more of the devils rushed from the water downstream. Gaining speed, they crashed into the first barrier, where they were impaled on the pointed spears of the fence.

Unaffected by their horrendous wounds, the demons were nonetheless caught on the barbed points, wrenching against their firm wooden bonds as they tried to break free.

To the north, several more beasts emerged from the dark water, moving fast and with discouraging dexterity. The sound of two musket blasts accompanied their advance, and one of them stepped to the side, missing half its neck. The devil stumbled awkwardly, like it was performing a bizarre dance, before collapsing into the shallow water.

The muddy shore in front of the spear-tipped barriers soon filled with yet more figures. They made no sound as they yanked on the thickets, trying to move the firmly set obstacles.

In time, their vile hands tugged harder on the impromptu fences, managing to yank them partially out of their crude foundations.

With a rush, three of the dreadful attackers leapt one of the fences, crashing into the second barrier with jarring force. Impaled, two of them struggled against the secondary impediment, while the third was unmoving, as a sharp stick was spiked neatly through its eye and out the back of its head.

More booms from the soldiers' weapons filled the night, but in a worrying sight, only a few of the hideous demons were felled during their onslaught. Meanwhile, more of their hellish brethren emerged from the river.

Directly in front of Hakan, five of the possessed creatures began wading through the water, looking directly at him as they sloshed through the current. They did not rush blindly at the chief, but approached methodically, like he was a cornered rat. The swooshing movements of their legs pressed through the current, moving eagerly forward to finish their cornered foe.

"Aiiiiiiiyeeeahhhhh," screamed Hakan as he challenged the attacking devils with a piercing war whoop.

The unholy assailants focused even more on Hakan, gaining speed as they exited the rapids. Moving quickly, they ran toward the narrow opening between the spear-tipped fences, where Hakan waited only a few yards beyond.

Getting close to their goal, the fetid monsters disappeared with a crash into a hidden pit between the barriers.

What was before a trench covered in loose branches was now a mass of writhing creatures. They lay on a host of sharpened spikes, struggling to various degrees after being skewered on the sharp points of multiple sharpened stakes.

Their limbs and torsos pulled against the spikes like a roiling mass of mating snakes, but no moan or cry of pain emerged from their fetid mouths.

Striding forward, Hakan took his chance to finish them off. Rearing back, he plunged his spear into their exposed heads, ramming his weapon repeatedly through their repulsive skulls in quick succession. When the last was destroyed and still, Hakan grinned in brief triumph.

Rising to his full height, Hakan stared across the river to the elevated heights that looked down from the opposing tree line. Chindi stood there underneath a stand of tall trees, where he oversaw the battle below. The demon leader's shadowed form peered down at Hakan, unmoving and quiet.

Hakan recognized him and pointed his bloody spear at Chindi, beckoning him with a boisterous challenge. "Come to me, devil. Don't hide like a scared squaw."

Chindi wasn't interested in the challenge, and he didn't move to join the melee. Instead, his possessed brother Billy walked to his side and stared down at Hakan. Billy took a keener interest in Hakan's provocative demand for battle, and he stepped deliberatively down the hill, moving carefully toward the river and the waiting chief.

Against the backdrop of booming muskets and the frantic pushing of demonic creatures against the weakening barriers, the water and shore filled with ever more attackers.

In front of Chindi, his remaining horrid force moved into the river, advancing forward to snuff out the desperate defenders. Chindi was now left alone on the heights, overlooking the developing fight like a hellish general overseeing his finest engagement.

As Billy moved to the rapids opposite Hakan, the chief muttered under his breath as he scanned the darkish area behind Chindi.

"Now, Crook. NOW!"

Behind Chindi, a figure unwound from a large tree branch and dropped quietly to the ground. Crook crouched silently, staring at the back of the rancid devil. Gathering his courage, he rubbed the white beads of Hakan's jewelry between his fingers, hoping the power of the charmed necklace cloaked him still.

Standing erect, Crook stepped carefully, approaching Chindi and sighting down his revolver. Foot over foot, he crept closer, aiming at the back of the possessed leader's head.

In front of Hakan, Billy faced him across the river. Striding into the rapids, the wretched monster sloshed quickly toward the chief.

Billy's gray skin shone under the pale moonlight, and his wicked eyes seemed to glow as he rushed to meet Hakan.

Around Hakan, the periodic blasts of muskets were not holding back the rest of the otherworldly assailants. On both sides, the creatures had managed to move the initial barriers aside, despite their numerous dead compatriots lying sprawled across the muddy earth.

Billy arrived at the trench in front of Hakan, moving his gaze down to the destroyed devils lying in heaps on the spikes below. Carefully skirting the pit, he deftly jumped to the side and around it.

Rushing forth, Billy swung a vicious and bloody tomahawk at the chief. Surprised by the speed of the attack, Hakan was just able to parry the blow, but his crude spear snapped in the process.

The chief stumbled back, drawing his wicked knife and backing toward his pile of other pole weapons.

Billy pressed the attack, swinging the tomahawk in sweeping arcs, wielding it like a trained and unnatural axe man.

Behind the large barricade, Loraine saw Hakan being overwhelmed. He motioned to the ongoing fight while shouting to O'Rourke and Trumain. "Shoot the one who's fighting Hakan."

Surprised, Trumain glanced over to Loraine with a confused and unspoken question: *Why?*

Appearing as if he didn't know himself, Loraine shrugged and aimed his revolver through the wood barricade.

Frustrated, Loraine muttered under his breath. "I can't get a clear shot. Move out of the way, Chief…"

On the hill, Crook moved ever closer to Chindi's unsuspecting back. He aimed carefully, focusing down the revolver's simple sight with forced deliberation.

The crack of the weapon preceded the bullet striking Chindi's lower skull, blowing off a chunk of white bone. Chindi spun around, glaring at Crook with surprise and unrestrained hate.

Crook rapid-fired the revolver, fanning the hammer in five successive blasts. Each bullet struck Chindi, but the demon didn't fall, even while gore poured from holes in his face, neck and chest.

Near the river, Hakan was losing in his fight with the evil Billy. Hakan had several open wounds from slashes, and he was being harried by the relentless and never-tiring devil.

In defense, Hakan lunged, plunging his makeshift spear into Billy's neck. Unfortunately, the tip broke off with a snap in the devil's rigid flesh.

Moving quickly, Hakan flipped his knife in the air, catching it overhand and moving to ram it into one of Billy's pupil-less eyes.

Before he could attack, Billy threw his own tomahawk overhand, and it caught the chief in the neck with a *thunk*.

Stumbling backward, Hakan dropped his blade while grabbing at the stuck weapon. Falling to one knee, he slowly collapsed near the fire with the weapon still embedded in his throat.

"Father," yelled Nayeli, and she dropped her loading supplies and ran from the cover of the barricade. Loraine followed her out, holding up his revolver as she ran to Hakan.

Loraine fired several times and was joined by Trumain and O'Rourke, who also leveled and discharged their muskets.

Billy stumbled backward, and each bullet blew a jagged hole in his dark skin. He almost seemed confused at being attacked, and his gaze stared accusingly at Loraine as the sergeant strode toward him.

His revolver empty, Loraine kicked Billy into the pit, where the devil fell and was pierced with numerous spikes. As black blood flowed from his wounds, Billy fought to free himself from his pointed shackles.

Up on higher ground, Chindi's dead face stared at Crook oddly, like he knew something Crook didn't. A vague and evil smile crossed his lips, and the critically wounded devil took a defiant step toward Crook.

Crook lowered and holstered his revolver. Steeling himself, he drew his saber and paced toward Chindi. Swinging his sharp blade in a wide arc, he managed to pierce the neck of the creature, but Chindi took no other action to stop the attack.

As Crook swiped again and again, the devil accepted the blows, not fighting the assault.

Crook was growing tired after several more swipes of his sword. Rearing back, he finally decapitated the monster, and its body and head fell separately into the sparse shrubs of the hillside.

There now arose a sound from Chindi's mouth, the same demonic chorus that took Pugh near the creek. The same sound from Fort Hollenbush, when most of his men were killed or taken by the devils. It was the same maddening, soulless shrieking, but now it was of an even higher and more intense tone.

It was like a choir of tormented souls heard from afar, but getting closer, and it wanted Crook to be part of its vile legion…it wanted the lieutenant to join it…to command it.

Crook dropped his sword and stumbled to the body. Stepping haltingly, Crook grabbed Chindi's head. Leaning down, he grasped the torso by its suspenders and began dragging it toward the river.

The corpse of the demon had the bizarre Indian satchel affixed to it, and Crook yanked and pulled the corrupted body into the water. Step by torturous step, he moved through the rapids toward his companions and the burial ground on the other side of the river.

Around Loraine, the siege of demons was collapsing around them. The thickets are almost pushed aside, and Loraine faced toward the crowd of ogling devils as they prepared to break free from the last barriers.

"Don't let them take you alive," shouted Loraine, spinning around and reloading his revolver.

Grimacing at his side, Trumain and O'Rourke held up their bayonet-tipped muskets, preparing to make their last stand.

From the rapids, Crook emerged, dragging the dead weight of Chindi's corpse and carrying the head by its ratty hair. The demon's mouth was open, and the demonic serenade continued unabated.

Crook bled from the ears as he stumbled ahead. Madness clawed at his features, and he compelled his mind to assert its will against the power of the demon. Grudgingly, he forced his limbs to move with each step, struggling to maintain his thoughts as he concentrated.

Grunting with the effort, Crook heaved the body portion of Chindi into the pit, where it thudded next to his still-wriggling brother. As he held the head up to do the same, the devilish and loud maw called to him, begging Crook to join it.

Crook stumbled, dropping the head to the ground. He stared around, not knowing where he was or what was happening. His eyes glossed over and started to turn white as his foe found its way into his thoughts.

"Arrrrrrgggggghhhhh," yelled Crook, losing control over his own mind.

Crook grabbed at his ears, trying to force away the voices that seduced his internal conceptions of self. Flailing inside, he was fighting a losing battle, and he began changing physically, with his flesh abruptly turning a shade darker.

Near the fire, Nayeli stood from her wounded father and ran to the edge of the pit. She screamed across it to Crook, her fierce eyes meeting his. "Crook, we are here with you. Fight the demon."

Her caring features tried to reach through the hellish chorus, to overcome Chindi's evil attraction. Through sheer force of will, her powerful lungs called out, begging Crook to return to himself.

For a moment, her voice and intent overcame the pull of the wicked Chindi, and Crook's eyes returned to self-awareness.

With a wrenching scream, Crook stepped above the head and drove his booted heel into its wretched features. He kicked down several more times, and each assault on the horrific face lessened the maddening sound.

As the facial structures of Chindi broke down, the demonic wailing died away, and after more smashing by his heavy boot, the pulped head resembled nothing human.

With a final triumphant scream, Crook kicked the head into the spiked pit with its vile owner.

Looking up, Crook glared at the devils that surrounded and pulled on the last of the spiked fences. In unison, they stopped heaving against the tattered wooden pickets.

The collection of wicked creatures, standing in a moment of silence, slumped suddenly to the ground, their evil energy uniformly extinguished.

Chapter 11

The morning was pleasant, with the clear sky illuminating the lonely burial ground on the remote river shore. Smoke drifted into the sky from the remains of the still-burning bonfires used during the night.

Mounds of blackened corpses, the remains of the demons, were piled at various points on the shoreline. The flames of their pyres still licked at the mostly skeletal remains, and the former demons seemed to smile at their newly realized fate of just being dead.

The sun shone on the isolated stretch of river, but the cold was biting, causing the exhausted party to don all of their muddied and tattered clothing. They pulled the collars of their weathered uniforms tight around their necks, but their eyes were elsewhere as they came to terms with their horrific experiences.

Walking to the icy-cold shallows of the trickling rapids, Loraine looked down and sighed. Reaching into the water, he picked up the body of a former demon, gently carrying it to one of the crematory fires.

Loraine cast Nicholas into the burgeoning flames, where fire quickly took hold and burned away the remainder of his blue vest and britches. Loraine watched the unseen body as it was consumed, and the normally impassive sergeant trembled from something more than the cold.

Near the main fire close to the river, Nayeli sat with Hakan, cradling him in her lap. He was bandaged and bloody but kept warm and comfortable with his daughter's comforting touch.

Hakan's face was pasty white as he stared up at Nayeli. He was fading from life, but his eyes were aware and engaged. He spoke in his native tongue, forcing his words through his acute pain.

"It has not been an easy life, daughter," Hakan whispered. *"I always sought to do the best for you and our people, but I fear I...chose wrong."*

Tears welled up in Nayeli's eyes, and one dropped on Hakan's cheek as she stared down.

"What is done cannot be undone, Father," Nayeli replied. *"Even when we do horrible things, we can always be forgiven in the spirit world. This is the way of the Great Spirit."*

Hakan nodded, his eyes hopeful. *"That is the way of things, but I ask you something before I go. A favor for your stubborn father."*

Nayeli nodded, her tears flowing freely.

"Bury me with my ancestors here, so that I can be with them," Hakan said, coughing and forcing air into his depleted lungs. *"As time passes, we will always hunt here in our ancient land, without loss or sadness."*

Nayeli moved her head intensely in agreement, and her voice cracked in grief. *"Father, I will miss you. "Watch over me with our ancestors. Help me to make the right choices in my life, especially when they are most important."*

Hakan nodded and smiled, even as he labored for air.

From behind Nayeli, a hand fell on her shoulder. Looking up, she saw Crook's face, full of worry and compassion. Crook didn't speak, but neither did he need to. Standing quietly, he squeezed her shoulder with acute empathy for both her and her father.

Hakan saw the unspoken exchange, and he nodded his approval up at Crook. As he struggled for breath, his gaze drifted between his daughter and the lieutenant.

As his strained breaths continued, his eyes peered into the sky, searching for something. Focusing on an unseen goal, he seemed to find what he was looking for, and a brief smile crossed his lips.

With a final gasp, Hakan died.

Nayeli rocked the chief's body, and she chanted in mourning as she looked down at his peaceful face. Crook kept his hand on her, patting her back as she wept openly.

Around her and Crook, the rest of the party gathered their equipment and belongings, preparing for yet another journey.

#

The forest trail descended along an extended path, twisting through frosty trees and iced-over brush. The ground to both sides of the path was covered by light snow.

Far ahead, there were less trees and more warmth as the mountainous environment gave way to the more moderate climate of California's Central Valley.

The group of four soldiers and one Native hiked down the frozen path, and plumes from their icy breaths rose into the crisp morning air. The ground crunched under every step, making travel difficult for the disheveled party in their worn-out shoes and moccasins.

Crook and Nayeli walked in the lead, but they were not in a hurry as they studied the icy ground and scattered bushes near the trail.

Stopping, Nayeli leaned against Crook for support, who was equally exhausted and cold. Looking fondly at one another, their growing affection was sealed by their shared and frightful experiences.

Behind them, Loraine turned his tobacco over in his cheek, looking impatient and frowning. Forever sullen, he looked like he could hike for a week longer without breaking a sweat.

At the back of the line, Trumain and O'Rourke clutched their muskets, sufficiently tired and hungry that it appeared they would soon be unable to carry their weapons. Staring blankly ahead, they waited for some respite from the marching and fighting they had grown so accustomed to, and neither of the surviving privates seemed capable of a smile.

For a considerable time, the group made the same pace as they moved ahead. Their wooden movements matched the cold weather, with their joints not appearing to cooperate with their intentions to make a normal pace.

The monotonous trek continued without speech or talking by the companions. With only the occasional chattering of birds, there was little sound to accompany their timid steps.

Ahead, the ground grew flatter, and the woods became less numerous. The trail widened, and they continued their less-than-brisk way ahead. With fatigued and weary expressions, they plodded on, hoping there was a light at the end of their long and sad expedition.

As the party rounded a curve in the trail, Crook and Nayeli stared ahead in surprise. Glancing between each other and to the other members behind, their eyes grew wide and exhilarated.

Ahead, a long column of soldiers advanced toward them. Scores of troopers with clean bearings and proper uniforms marched toward the bedraggled party, and the group stared open-mouthed in return.

One of the rider-messengers sent by Loraine from Fort Hollenbush was at the head of the column, and he waved at Crook with a relieved grin.

Near the head of the reinforcements was a covered wagon. Sitting next to the soldier driving the wagon were Henry and Bonnie Clayton, and they smiled genuinely at the party. Behind them, Sara peeked her head out and waved at the group.

Shocked and happy, Crook and Nayeli returned the wave, along with Trumain, O'Rourke, and even Loraine. The trauma of the survivors slipped away, if only for a brief while.

Crook offered Nayeli an inquisitive glance, confusion on his face.

Nayeli returned the look with a knowing smile and motioned toward the Claytons. "I told them: you give your life for your people, but even you had to flee Chindi. If even you must run away, giving up your fort and your men, then what good is it for them to die? I say to them, 'God want you to live for another day, for peace and to build life.' It is good they listened."

Crook nodded in understanding, even as he mulled over his decisions and losses from their long and demanding trek. Tentatively, he glanced back to his soldiers, who waved excitedly at the incoming group of fresh soldiers.

At long last, his men smiled with unrestrained happiness. Long-awaited relief showed on their faces, matching their feelings of hope for the uncertain future.

#

Pit River, Present Day

The flowing river was beautiful and calm, with the afternoon sun glistening on its subdued surface. Above, fluffy clouds shrouded the blue sky.

The open field around the waterway was quiet, except for the gentle swoosh of swaying grass from a mild and cool breeze.

The silence was broken by a backhoe starting its engine. As it revved and spat out a cloud of black smoke, the ponderous yellow machine began digging a trench near the waterline. With the cranking of its gears and hydraulics, it plucked dirt in great buckets, swiveling to deposit the results away from the river. The wide footing it carved in the moist earth ran parallel to the river.

Ayita Miller stood near the water, watching the loud digging with a contented expression. In her thirties and visibly pregnant, her remarkable features revealed her Native American heritage. Her long black hair swayed in a refreshing breeze, and she flicked it out of her eyes with an absent swipe of her hand. Transferring her gaze over the broad river, she could barely control her excitement.

Her husband Derek Miller stood at her side. Equally excited, Derek watched the unfolding excavation with open and thrilled features. He was white and middle aged, and his love for Ayita was evident in each adoring glance he cast her way.

Derek held up a set of building plans, following the expected outline of the ditch with his finger as he compared it to the representation on the plans. He glanced back and forth several times, confirming in his mind's eye the location of his living room and its captivating view over the river.

The backhoe stuttered for a moment, and its scooping digger caught on something below the surface. The engine died as the man inside the machine shut it down.

Opening his door, the burly backhoe operator stuck his head out, raising his voice to Derek as he pointed to the footing he had been digging. "I hit something down there. Take a look, would ya?"

Derek smiled, then shrugged and looked at his wife. His grin was infectious, and she returned it with equal intensity.

"We can't expect to build our dream home without a few hiccups," Derek said. "Hope we didn't hit some old graves; the tribe will shut us down for a month—or longer."

Ayita frowned at the thought, then nodded to the ditch in worried anticipation.

Derek walked over to the trench, setting the plans to the side. Jumping down, he fell to his knees and dug with his hands amongst the moist upturned earth.

"Hey, it's some kinda old Indian bag. Cool," Derek said, his manner becoming carefree and enthusiastic.

After a moment, Derek said nothing more, and he continued to stare down at the dark-brown soil.

Ayita walked over behind him, peering at his crouched back. Absently, she placed her hand flat across her neckline, where the white beads of ancient necklace were just visible beneath her fingers.

Abruptly, a strange and forceful gale picked up and howled with some power across the remote river. Ayita's disturbed glance moved to the increasing ripples of the wind-driven water, then back again to her silent husband. Perplexed, her gaze flitted down to the open ditch, searching for what was wrong.

Panic crept into Ayita's voice. "Derek...Derek, what is it?"

The End

About the Author

Tim lives in Nevada, where he makes a life enjoying all things horror-related, from films to books—and even the occasional convention. He has three children, two cats, and he enjoys providing reading entertainment for the monster and creature-loving masses.

If you like this novel, he would appreciate a review on Amazon or a follow on Facebook:

https://www.horrorthrillerguy.com/

For the opportunity to win free hardcover versions of this and all future books, please join his mailing list:

https://mailchi.mp/143ae89c5418/horrorthrillerguy

Also by Timothy Bryan:

The Huntsman of Corvinus
books2read.com/u/mVRyr5

Despicable
books2read.com/u/49k0ak

By Their Cold Fingers
books2read.com/u/bPgMKr

Core Ruleset
books2read.com/u/mqXyQ6

Prisoners of a Dark Night
books2read.com/u/mIIzqW